# The Forest Queen

# The Forest Queen

## BETSY CORNWELL

CLARION BOOKS
Houghton Mifflin Harcourt
Boston   New York

Clarion Books
3 Park Avenue
New York, New York 10016

Clarion Books is an imprint of Houghton Mifflin Harcourt Publishing Company.

hmhco.com

The text was set in Adobe Garamond Pro.
Interior art copyright © 2018 by Sarah J. Coleman

*Library of Congress Cataloging-in-Publication Data*
Names: Cornwell, Betsy, author.
Title: The Forest Queen / Betsy Cornwell.
Description: Boston ; New York : Clarion Books, Houghton Mifflin Harcourt,
[2018] | Summary: A retelling of Robin Hood in which Lady Silviana of Loughsley
joins her childhood friend Bird, Little Jane, Mae Tuck, and others to become an
outlaw fighting for social justice against her brother John, the Sheriff.
Identifiers: LCCN 2017036566 | ISBN 9780544888197 (hardback : alk. paper)
Subjects: | CYAC: Robbers and outlaws—Fiction. | Nobility—Fiction. | Sex role—
Fiction. | Middle Ages—Fiction. | Love—Fiction. | Sherwood Forest (England)—
Fiction. | Great Britain—History—John, 1199–1216—Fiction.
Classification: LCC PZ7.C816457 For 2018 | DDC [Fic]—dc23
LC record available at https://lccn.loc.gov/2017036566

Manufactured in the United States of America
DOC 10 9 8 7 6 5 4 3 2 1
4500720986

*For D.S.E.L.,*
*whose middle name is Sherwood*

Thus ev'ry kind their pleasure find,
The savage and the tender;
Some social join, and leagues combine,
Some solitary wander:
Avaunt, away! The cruel sway,
Tyrannic man's dominion;
The sportsman's joy, the murd'ring cry,
The flutt'ring, gory pinion!
— "Song Composed in August"
Robert Burns, 1783

# Prologue

High in the trees of Woodshire Forest on a sunny day, the light doesn't seem to come from above you at all. Light springs out of the leaves there, a round robin of tree and sky: it streams off every twig, drips into the edges of each ebbing shadow until the whole canopy floods with gold, until the air itself smells like light, bittersweet and fresh. You can drown in green sunshine up there.

Bird and I used to swim in it every day. We'd climb the trees right up to the very top, or at least, as close as we could get. As we grew older, the young branches on the treetops started snapping under our weight. By the time we were ten we couldn't quite get above the canopy anymore.

I was bigger than Bird then, and I always told him he should still go up without me. But he never did.

"Why climb a tree at all if you won't go as high as you can?" I asked him the first few times. He just grinned at me.

Eventually I stopped asking. In truth, I'd have missed

him if he'd climbed higher than I could follow; he was always my favorite company, and I his. Like trees and sunshine, Bird and me, although I couldn't tell you who was which.

I think that's what bothered John first — long before he took over the estate, before he became sheriff or tried to marry me off or anything else that happened. Just that I preferred Bird to him.

John never climbed the trees with us. But sometimes he would wait on the ground as we climbed, and I could feel his gaze on the backs of my legs, watching.

*Autumn*

# ~ONE~

## *Chasing the Hart*

The huntswoman sounded her horn, and hounds rushed like water around our horses' feet.

I leaned forward over my mare's neck and let out a steady breath as we jumped the stream. She landed lightly, our speed barely breaking, and we plunged ahead with the rest of the party.

I heard a falcon's cry and looked back just in time to see the great raptor spread her wings and push off from Bird's leather-gloved hand. Seraph flashed into the green ocean above us and my friend grinned, tucking the falcon's hood into his sleeve.

I felt the huge muscles under me tighten and I looked ahead to see the fallen tree my horse was about to jump. This time I wasn't ready, and I had my breath knocked from me on her landing as punishment. One of her ears flicked back in reassurance or annoyance, and I felt a reminding tug on the reins I always kept as loose as I could. *Pay attention,* she was saying. *You're not sitting in any rocking chair, here.*

Bowstrings sliced across my chest as I leaned forward again. I pressed my legs more firmly against the mare's side and slid my hands into her mane. She felt my focus and began to run flat out.

Soon all I could see were flashing, flickering streaks of green and orange, the forest colors around us flaming toward autumn. The day was crisp, September-cool, but inside my wool riding habit I was beginning to sweat.

Scenthounds bayed just ahead of us. The riders gave out joyful whoops and warrior cries. Close behind me on his red-roan gelding, Bird was silent, but I could feel him, focused and determined, listening for the falcon that rode the wind above us, far beyond the shifting, murmuring canopy.

Then, with a shock like plunging into cold water, we left the forest shadows and entered a sunny clearing, an expanse of tall grass and daisies with a sheer cliff on the other side. There, trapped against the rockface, stood the hart we chased.

His antlers betrayed his age: no young buck he, but a great elder king of the forest, his horns twisting into a crown that nearly doubled his considerable height. He stomped and thrust those antlers bravely forward, menacing us, but he knew well that he was trapped.

He'd have to be old to be caught, I knew. Young and healthy quarry, whether hart or hare, fox or boar, almost always outran the hounds. I'd been on countless hunts, and only a handful of times had our day of riding and jumping and following the graceful calls of hound and horn yielded any actual meat for the Loughsley table.

But this day, it would. I sent up a heartfelt prayer for this animal's quick, clean death, now that at last we had it cornered.

"Hold!"

The hounds hung back, corralled in an instant by the huntswoman's calls. In the wild, the pack would have overwhelmed this beast in an instant, but a formal hunt is different.

I tugged my mare's reins, even though she was already coming to a stop. Shifting the balance of my waist and hips in the sidesaddle, I straightened my spine as I pulled the bow from my back.

Prince Rioch moved for his crossbow. As the highest-ranking hunter, the prince had the honor of the first shot, but all of us would be ready to dispatch the animal quickly if his aim faltered. Any good hunter spares their prey need-less pain.

He raised his arms and squared his shoulders, settling the heft of the crossbow in his hands. He squinted through the precisely carved notch at its center.

Beside him my brother, John, watched and nodded his encouragement. This was our young royal's first time hunting without the king: he'd never had first shot before.

The prince's arrow flew across the clearing.

I felt a familiar shadow pass over me, and without looking up I knew that Bird's falcon circled us, and that she watched the arrow, too.

It pierced the hart's hind leg.

He gave a guttural, frothy scream that turned into a panicked groan as he tried to run and found that he could not.

Hobbled, the great stag began a struggling limp toward the forest.

I raised my bow, taking in the long breath that would allow me, on the exhale, to shoot clean and true. Around me two dozen hunters did the same. All of us watched the huntswoman from the corners of our eyes; she would give the signal that would let us end the beast's suffering, and she would not wait long to do it.

The huntswoman raised her horn.

"Wait!" John called.

I stared at my brother in horror.

"It is the prince's first quarry," he said. "Let him try again."

I looked back at the huntswoman. I was certain she wouldn't let this stand; she was a clean and rigorous hunter, and I knew the worth she saw in each life her hunting parties took. She was Bird's mother, for goodness' sake!

But she moved the curved horn away from her tight-set lips and nodded.

Behind me I heard Bird's strangled breath. Both he and the huntswoman were servants of Loughsley, and they could not contradict its young master; and even though I was its lady, as the younger sibling, I had no more authority to speak over my brother than they did. Besides, our visiting monarch had just named John sheriff; John had even more power now.

The prince took out another arrow. He fumbled at his crossbow with unpracticed hands.

After a long minute, John took the bow and reloaded for him. He handed the crossbow back to our prince with a dutiful nod.

"Thank you, Loughsley," Rioch muttered, his color rising.

*Don't bother with thanks,* I thought. *Just kill the poor thing.*

The prince's second shot hit the stag in the neck. Too high to break his windpipe or open an artery, too low to pierce the spine and cease his pain.

The sound he made this time wasn't panicked or even loud. It was mewling. Low. He leaned to one side, giving slow, panting, bubbling breaths. His tongue began to loll even while his eyes stayed open.

His punctured leg buckled, and with a faint snap, he fell.

Still the huntswoman watched my brother.

"Once more, Your Highness," John said.

The prince's face was red. "I'll reload myself," he muttered.

In time ticked out by the wheezing clock of the hart's wounded breaths, he did so.

A lean, brindled sighthound at the front of our party whined at the scent of blood. I heard the soft clashing of feathers behind me: the falcon came to rest on Bird's arm again. The twenty or so humans all stayed as still as the animals, our hands cautious on bows, or tight on bridles or saddle horns.

None of them would speak against my brother, let alone the prince.

And the beast at the edge of the cliff lay trapped. Killed already, or as good as, but not yet dead, the animal panic in him not enough to numb his pain or mend his bones or carry him to safety.

I raised my bow again and shot him through the heart.

# ~TWO~

## The Hunt Ball

One person at the ball was speaking to me at least.

"Honestly, Silvie, I don't know how you can bear it," murmured Lady Clara Halving, smoothing her yellow skirts with one hand and reaching into her long bell sleeve with the other. She produced her nonsensically tiny dog, Titan, and stroked him under the chin. "Hurting innocent animals like that." She held Titan up to her face and cooed.

The dog blinked lazily and came halfway out of his drugged stupor. He gave a yawn and displayed a curling pink tongue the size of a fingernail.

I had to admit, he was adorable.

Still. "Honestly, Clara, I don't know how *you* can bear it," I replied coolly, "keeping Titan so tranced on opiates he's more a stuffed toy than a dog. It's animal cruelty."

She huffed and drew herself up to her full height, which wasn't much; her lovely eyes flashed. "I'd never hurt a fly, let alone my sweet puppy," she informed me, stuffing Titan back up her sleeve. "I give him the drops for his anxiety, poor dear!" She stalked away in the direction of the buffet table.

"Off for more venison?" I called after her, annoyed — but at myself, really, not her. Clara had been kind to talk with me. She'd clearly heard the story of my killing the hart, and had known well that it would do her no favors to be seen speaking with me. Like so many young noblewomen, she still cherished a hope of attracting Prince Rioch . . . whom I had flagrantly embarrassed mere hours earlier.

Lord, it had been romantic suicide for her to speak to me at all. And even though we had some differing opinions, that was hardly reason for me to intentionally push away such selflessness — especially when almost all the courtiers kept their pets drugged, to stop them from biting or yipping or generally causing a fuss the way animals do. Even the prince kept his dog, a squat and bleary-eyed hound, on the drops. Rioch scratched the dog's head absent-mindedly as yet another nobleman approached him to tell pretty lies about his hunting prowess, his bravery, his wisdom in appointing my brother as sheriff. There could be no greater lie than calling it wise to give John power.

I rushed after Clara and touched her shoulder. When she turned, still haughty, I dropped a quick curtsey and then looked her straight in the eye.

"I'm sorry, Clara, truly," I said. "Please, I know you were being kind."

"Was I?" A muscle in her neck twitched. "And I thought someone just told me I was cruel." But then she sighed. "Never mind. You were right about the venison, at least. I can't resist it, and where do I think it comes from?"

I had to keep myself from embracing her. "I was trying to end the hart's suffering. The prince couldn't . . ." I trailed off, not wanting to offend her again by speaking ill of Rioch.

"That fool? If he can't aim for the plum target right in front of him at court"—she tapped her bosom and gave me a too-innocent look—"one can't expect his arrows to hit the side of a castle, never mind some little old deer."

I giggled, grateful for the change of subject. "You've given up all hope, then?"

She shrugged. "I've developed a taste for the palace guards," she said with a mischievous smile. "They've bigger muscles than the noblemen, except of course for new sheriffs who spend their days beating people up—" We both realized she meant my brother in the same moment, and Clara colored and quickly moved on. "Rioch's never looked twice at even the foreign royals who get shipped in to woo him—like that Su princess, Ghazia, who's here now—let alone any Estinger. If you ask me, he doesn't believe there's a girl on the three continents who's good enough for him. I think his upcoming voyage is just to get away from us." She threw up her hands dramatically.

A drunken yip came from her sleeve. "Ooh, sorry, Titan!" Clara petted and fretted over the dog. When he'd settled himself to sleep again, she looked me up and down. "I do love your gown, Silvie, and you're doing it justice. You'd be quite the success if you ever bothered to come to court, you know, and there are others besides our head-in-the-clouds prince who are well worth attracting. Lord Danton, for one." She winked again.

I winced, as if on cue. Five years ago, the last time Loughsley Abbey had hosted a Hunt Ball, I had admired Lord Danton quite ardently—and I'd blathered about my crush to every other young girl there. Knowing nothing of palace gossip or fashion or tiny lap dogs, I was just grateful to have something to talk about with them.

Of course, the result was that every soul at the party knew about my infatuation within the hour—Lord Danton included. He'd indulgently asked me for a waltz, but when I'd seen his knowing smile I had run away, mortified, and hidden myself in the garden for the rest of the night.

Clara had brought it all back with humiliating clarity. It was almost as hard to forgive her that harmless teasing as her comments about the hunt.

But I gritted my teeth; unlike five years ago, I was determined not to mind what anyone thought of me. "I wish I could, Clara. And thank you. You look beautiful, too."

I smoothed my skirts, managing a little smile. My dress was pale green with a white silk bodice panel and a delicate gold lattice crossed over the full skirt. "Your cage gown," the seamstress had called it with a laugh quickly followed by a stricken look, wondering if she'd caused offense. But the idea had appealed to me: after all, it wasn't entirely untrue. I had lived my whole life at Loughsley Abbey in just such a beautiful green-and-gold cage.

I'd been born in the room I still slept in now. Tutors and governesses had been imported all the way from Esting City, had made the long trek around the wilds of the forest to come here and teach me to dance and ride sidesaddle and hold my forks correctly. My father had taught both John and me to read and write. John had gone to the palace when he was twelve, but I never had. When he was preparing to leave and my father asked me, at age nine, if I would like to go, too, I had been overcome with an attack of shyness so severe that I could hardly breathe, let alone speak. I only shook my head no. John had told me all about the courtiers' children, and how bullying and mean they were, and warned me that I should stay away for my own safety.

Neither of us had left the estate grounds before. It was only after he was gone that I wondered how he'd known himself.

But John must have been right, because he came back even crueller than he'd been before. The highborn thugs who started visiting him here were meaner than the village bullies he'd once corralled, too.

So I'd been happy enough to stay tucked away in Loughsley, our beautiful home perched between rock and water, the great forest wrapped around us like so many green blankets. I'd always been a quiet child, and I spent my time plunging into my lessons, practicing the music of my lap harp or the steps of my dances. I would read or embroider or walk in the garden, reciting the names of all the herbs and flowers there, and their uses, when I knew them. That last I might not have been expected to know, but the tutor who'd introduced me to botany thought that ladies should not just know enough about plants to arrange them into lovely bouquets, but to understand their more practical uses, too. More than once I'd gone to the gardens to chew peppermint for an aching stomach, when something John had done or Father had forgotten to do had made my insides churn with worry. And when that was not enough, there was always, always Bird: always the healing kindness we both found inside our friendship. Climbing trees together, surveying the infinite green of the canopy and talking softly as leaves and breezes murmured around us, felt grander than any court life I could imagine.

I'd have no solitude for picking peppermint, no quiet

greenery, no private garden, no Bird at all, if I went to the palace.

So I was half lying when I told Clara I wished I could come to court. The idea still frightened me.

Still, part of me did wish to be part of, if not the city and the palace, some kind of greater, brighter world . . .

"Silviana!"

I shook myself. "Yes?" I asked Clara.

She shook her head. Her expression had changed, gone closed off. It wasn't she who had spoken.

I turned to see what she was staring at, for she would not look at me.

My brother stood with Lord Danton, beckoning me forward.

❧ ❧

My heart was breaking.

I collapsed onto Bird's secret chair and buried my face in my hands, until the weight of all the hair piled atop my head threatened to pull me forward and out of my seat entirely. I should never have chosen such an elaborate style, even if the pain of the pulling and weaving of all those tight braids had distracted me from bigger problems.

I forced my hands down from my face.

*Don't think about it. Don't think about it. Forget.*

I focused on what I could see: there were dark

suggestions of brambles and flowers in front of me, interlocking branches of the pine and chestnut trees beyond, and bright spangles of stars, fractured through the tears in my eyes, overhead.

With my next deep breath I could taste the greenery that surrounded me: the grass, the roses and lilies and morning glories climbing the more dignified part of my father's overgrown, once-beloved gardens. The patch of peppermint that I ate from nearly every day.

I leaned back, and cool stone caught me. It had been years and years since Bird built this little hideaway, and months and months since I'd come here, but I'd never felt more grateful for it. It was like a little wild fort, just beyond the borders of Loughsley Abbey's vast gardens. I didn't think John knew about it, or even the gardeners; they never bothered to come out this far anymore. No one did. Just Bird and me.

I tucked my feet up under my legs. They'd already gone cold in my thin, soft dancing shoes; even though summer was barely over, the night air was cool.

I pulled a handkerchief out of my bodice and mopped my face, then forcefully blew my nose.

John always said doing that made me sound like a man.

But then, he said the same thing when I talked too much, or walked too quickly—stomped, he said—or, really, when I did anything that differentiated me from one of the singing wind-up dolls Father used to give me. John liked to think of himself as the man of the house, and strangely enough, he seemed to believe I could infringe on that.

John was the one who ordered the servants around, who decided how much to tax our estate's tenants, and who sent those taxes on to the king. It had been a few years since Father had been well enough to do such things himself. John was the one, these days, whom people called simply Loughsley . . . although they'd have to start calling him Sheriff now.

I shivered.

I could still picture him in the ballroom I'd just left, resplendent in his red velvet half cape, smiling in just the right way to set off his wide, square jawline. A cloud of noblewomen floated around him, waiting, wanting. He'd beckoned me with such assurance, the way a hero from a storybook might. My brother looked more like a prince than Rioch did.

I could already see that he was going to tell me something I wouldn't like, and he was going to tell me in a loud voice, with plenty of important people nearby who would expect me to give the answer John wanted me to give. He was going to say it in a way that would keep me from saying no.

I felt sick. I always felt sick when I had to be anywhere near my brother. He hadn't hit me in years, hadn't hurt me at all since I was twelve, and yet the feeling had grown worse and worse.

*Don't think about it. Don't think about it. Forget.*

I made myself walk toward him.

John went back to talking with his friends as I approached. He was boasting about what he'd be able to do now that he was sheriff: his first project, he was saying loudly, would be to reopen the parts of Esting City's prison that had been unused for over a century. "We've been too lenient with our criminals, and especially with our debtors," he was saying. "Stricter enforcement is the first order of business, of course. We need to make people really *afraid* of not paying their taxes. The local jails are serviceable, but they don't engender enough fear. Do you know they have iron maidens in the old prison? Those would make you hand over some coins, I'd imagine." His friends laughed. "A few oubliettes, too. It's about time we put our country's resources to use."

I stared at him. I'd known, understood in some bone-deep part of me for all my life how cruel he was, but . . . iron maidens and oubliettes were torture, old methods of dealing out slow, horrible deaths that I'd only read about in books. The first was a metal coffin lined with spikes, the second a bottle-shaped prison cell dug into the ground, where men were thrown and left until they starved or went mad. Our country had abandoned such barbaric practices centuries earlier. I could not quite believe that even my bully brother would want to bring them back.

I heard derisive giggling from behind me, near the staircase.

John froze; his broad smile vanished.

I turned to where he was looking, and I saw our father.

The real Lord Loughsley was blinking in the entrance to the ballroom. He stood tall and straight, wearing the beautiful old silvery military coat from his campaigns of fifty years before. His color was good; looking at his face, one would have thought he was in perfect health. His eyes were perhaps slightly less focused than they'd been a year or so earlier, when I'd still managed to tell myself that there was nothing wrong with him.

His feet were bare. His beautiful coat almost covered the nightshirt that brushed against his naked knees.

My father smiled. "Welcome, honored guests," he intoned. He bowed, first straight ahead and then to each side of the room, showing the backs of his thighs to the assembled crowd. He wobbled on the last bow and nearly fell, but straightened himself again.

Not everyone laughed, but I hated every single person who did.

I rushed toward him across the polished floor.

John whistled, the way he'd call for the hounds. Two footmen stepped out of the shadows and grabbed my father by the arms before I could reach him.

He frowned. "Let me go!" he said, but John was there already. He shook his head at the footmen, and there was no question whom the two men would obey.

"Don't worry, friends," John said. He turned toward our father. "Come now, you need to follow the dress code for occasions such as these. The *prince* is here." He spun gracefully around and made a flourishing bow to our young, mousy monarch, in whose honor John had given this Hunt Ball. When the courtiers' laughter started again, John laughed with them.

I saw the shame on my once-fastidious father's face as his servants hustled him out of the ballroom. My own face flamed with anger, and I felt my heartbeat quicken. I hurried after them.

But John caught me by the arm, just as roughly as his lackeys had done to my father.

"How could you embarrass him like that?" I hissed as he turned me forcibly around, his grin firmly back in place.

John glared. "Embarrass *him?*"

I tried to pull my arm away, but John was always boxing and wrestling with his friends, or with whichever servant happened to be nearby if his friends were unavailable; he was stronger than probably anyone else I knew, save Bird.

My tree-climbing and archery practice didn't give me the strength to match him. I could either let him lead me toward the center of the ballroom, or sink onto the floor and make a spectacle of myself, as John would say. And I knew what the result of that would be: more footmen, dragging me out of the room like a pet that had forgotten its house-training, just like they'd done to my father.

So I let John pull me forward. I saw Clara out of the corner of my eye, watching me pityingly, but she said nothing. And I couldn't blame her, either; no courtier's kindness, however genuine, could extend far enough to free me from my brother's grasp.

Was he taking me back to Rioch to apologize? I wondered.

No. Not to Rioch, and not to apologize.

He led me to Lord Danton instead.

And in that loud, proclamatory voice he said:

"My friend has made me an offer for you, Silviana, and I have accepted."

*Don't think about it.*

"What're you crying for, Silvie?"

A voice from above pulled me back to the garden.

Tears still spangled my vision, but when I looked up, the long, broad-shouldered form crouched on the branches was as familiar as ever. Even broken by teardrops; even in darkness.

A laugh leapt out of my throat. "No business of yours, dolt," I croaked. There were traces of crying still in my voice, too, but repeating the first words Bird and I had ever said to each other helped clear them away.

Just as he'd intended. I swiped at my eyes once more.

Bird landed on the ground as lightly as if he had wings after all. His light brown hair glinted with rain from the shower that had come down during the ball, while I was safe, or stuck, inside.

He shook his head, drops flying, and smiled at me. When I didn't respond, he bent down so our eyes were almost level.

"Go on, then, box my ears," he said, turning his head to offer them. "That's how this goes."

Another laugh came out of me all on its own. "I don't think I could take you on anymore, Bird. You're not so weak as you once were."

He snorted. "Weak, nothing! I was a fine young lad."

I was starting to smile back now; I couldn't help it. "The first time I saw you, you were the smallest, skinniest, most knobby-jointed little boy in the world. Staring at me with your big round eyes and asking me why I was crying and knowing my name, even though I didn't know yours."

"Ah, sure but that was only natural. You were the daughter of the house, and big and bright and beautiful besides, and I was merely the not-at-all-weak son of the new huntswoman. How could I have hoped that you'd know who I was?" He sighed dramatically, leaning against the nearest tree.

I tumbled smiling into the memory, just as he'd meant me to.

Of course I hadn't known his name. I was only five, I had never left the estate, and my big brother and his friends were always the foremost threats in my mind. I thought this stripling must surely be a new member of John's bully gang. I thought he must know my name because they'd sent him.

I was a sturdy type, even at five, and I saw an opportunity I hadn't had before: to ensure I was no longer the runt of the Loughsley litter.

*An ounce of prevention,* I lectured myself.

Then I boxed his ears.

He really had resembled a baby bird then — not the fluffy speckled chicks in the henhouse, but the ugly, scrawny, just-hatched blackbirds without their feathers that John and the boys had knocked out of their nest a few days before — and he squeaked when I boxed his ears, just the way the birds had when John had crushed them under his feet.

I suddenly saw the fragile, naked, bloody chicks as if it were they between my hands, and not this boy.

I stepped back. My fists had become John's, and not my own.

The skinny bird-boy was giving me such a look, too — it made me know at once that he was no ally of my brother's. He looked at me as if I had betrayed him. As if I were a fallen angel.

Only, I had never met him before, so that was impossible. How can you betray someone you don't even know? How can you fall from grace you never had?

And yet I wanted to make it up to him. I wanted my hands to be my own again, and not my brother's. I hated my brother's hands.

*Don't think about it.*

I reached out to the boy again, slowly, carefully. I hoped my face showed how I felt as clearly as his did.

I had only enough time to watch him flinch away from me, and to hate myself for it, before John and his friends came rollicking into the yard and descended upon us both.

Afterward, when the big boys had left, we patched each other up.

"How did you know my name, anyway?" I made sure to keep my voice gentle. John's beating had made it clear whose side we were both on.

He looked at me cautiously with his huge hazel eyes. "I didn't mean to make you angry, Silvie." He scrunched up his face, then corrected himself. "Mistress. I know your name because all of us do. My ma pointed you out the day we got here. She's the new huntswoman, and I'm going to learn to be her falconer. Only because of that and I'm so small, she calls me Bird. But it's Robert, really. Robert Falconer." He wrinkled up his face again. "Just in case you want to know. Which you probably don't."

"I do," I said. "And I wasn't angry . . ." I took a deep breath, feeling more foolish than ever. "I was scared."

He looked me up and down. Whatever eighteen-year-old Bird thought now, seven-year-old Bird had known how small he was. "Scared of *me?*"

I was at least a hand taller than Bird, and a stone heavier. It was fairly obvious who had more reason to be scared of whom.

He laughed, just a little unbelieving trill at first, but his laugh called mine to come out, too, and before I knew it we were both clutching our bellies and gasping for air and rolling around in the dust, mussing ourselves up again and not minding one bit.

We were seldom apart after that. If John and his cronies still found us all-too-easy targets for beating senseless, at least we could huddle together on the ground and protect each other's bellies from the worst of the blows.

It had been years since John had hit either of us, though. He left Bird well alone these days—as did most people— and he'd rarely even touched me since I was about twelve. When he did, it was with a kind of trembling gentleness, an extreme restraint that belied the violence, the . . . longing . . . that I so often saw in his eyes.

*Don't think about it.*

A cold breeze hissed over the garden, over Bird's secret chair, over my skin. I remembered Lord Danton's hand, reaching out to take mine. John's beatific smile behind him.

Thinking of that made the tears start again. I hiccupped and snorted, feeling ridiculous.

"Come now, Silvie," Bird said. "Tell me why you're crying, really. You do it so rarely anymore that I know it must be something serious."

He took my hand and pulled me out of the secret chair and up to my feet.

Our faces were very close. I could feel the warmth of his body, of his callused hand over mine. His nearness, his heat, was a balm. I leaned into him, and there was a calm, quieting feeling in my chest, like a bird touching down on the branch of a tree. I felt a pull like gravity tilting my face toward his.

He pulled away at once. "So," he said, eyes on the ground, "what was it?" And then, more gently, and looking at me: "What did he do this time?"

I flexed my now-empty hand and pulled my bell sleeve over it. When we were young enough to find boys or girls respectively disgusting, Bird and I had made one of the silly vows children make that we'd never kiss each other. The promise had irked me more than once since I'd noticed that I didn't find boys so horrible any longer . . . It bothered me more than it did him, I knew. But it had also kept us friends, and I valued *that* more than I did the lush warmth that rose in me when he was too near. So I kept our promise and never kissed him.

And I was grateful, I reminded myself, every time he pulled away when we got too close. Not disappointed, not frustrated. Grateful.

I took as deep a breath as I could between hiccups, and I told him the story of the Hunt Ball. Bird nodded in recognition when I mentioned this noble or that. When I told him about John whistling for the footmen as if they were dogs, he hissed softly. When I described how he had mocked our father, I saw him flinch.

"Lady and Lord!" Bird exclaimed. "If I were you, I'd have throttled him. Right then and there. In the ballroom, for everyone to see. Best if they did see!"

I knew he meant it. What was more, I knew that in a way, he thought less of me for *not* strangling my brother in the middle of the Hunt Ball. Bird was always so *visceral* about everything. Even when he was small—and up until a few years earlier he'd been very small—he was scrappy, determined, ruthless when he had to be. A true hunter.

He wasn't small anymore, but tall and broad, and those

big hazel eyes could flash with menace when they needed to. It was no wonder most people let him alone.

"But that wasn't the worst part," I said.

The worst was how in a way I thought less of me, too. Not of my failure to kill my brother—of course not—but of my failure to . . . to have subdued John somehow, to have stood up to him at some point before he brought us both to this moment, to this hunt, to this ball. To this revelation that I was not even a prize, which was enough to rail against, but simply a gift, a trinket, to be tossed to whomever my brother saw fit.

The fact that every other girl at the hunt had heard me admire Lord Danton years earlier only made it worse, somehow. John had used my own . . . longing . . . against me.

"I thought you liked Danton. Wasn't it good news?"

I shook my head. My braids were coming loose, and I felt the kinked loops of them brush my shoulders. My hair felt so heavy, as heavy as the world, as heavy as marriage. I reached up to pull out a pin, let down one braid; then I started on another.

"It might have been," I said, "some other way . . ." I sighed. "Not like this. Not at John's bidding. When I imagined a betrothal I always thought that he . . . that it would be *me* he'd want. Not because my brother made him some—some advantageous offer. One that conveniently leaves John as Loughsley's sole heir, and me thrown to the side, forgotten. Not that I don't wish sometimes that John would just forget me . . ."

I started pulling faster, scattering pins along the ground as we began to walk.

I thought distractedly of a tale one of my nurses had told about two children alone in the forest, leaving bread crumbs to mark their way back home. But birds had eaten the crumbs, and then the children had been lost indeed—at least until they came upon a house made of sweets in the heart of the wood.

My fingers caught in a braid. I tugged, but the motion only snared me tighter. I scrabbled at my head, feeling panic rise in my belly, feeling foolish that I would let so small a thing frighten me, but frightened nonetheless. Entangled. Trapped.

Bird reached up and stilled my hand. We both stopped walking. He unwove the snarl of hair. "You don't have to do what he tells you, you know," he said, laying the plaits neatly across my shoulder.

I turned away and started walking faster this time. "Don't condescend, Bird."

"I wasn't. Silvie, haven't you ever thought about—about just leaving? Leaving him?"

I flinched. "Leaving John? . . . Of course. But not my father. And not—not everyone else who lives at Loughsley, who lives on the tenanted land. I couldn't leave all of them to John's tender mercies, either."

"Even for the glorious Lord Danton?" He laughed.

I stopped and faced him full on. "Stop, Bird. Shut your mouth. You think you—you think you're so much tougher than I am, that you understand the world so much better, and I'm just some naive noble girl who can be led away from her family, from her duty, by a—by a silly crush. And I know that's all it was, thank you." I was breathing fast now. "You think you're so much stronger than I am, so much wiser, don't you?"

"Silvie, I—Silvie, I meant . . ." He took a deep breath. "Silvie, that's not what I'm trying to say." He looked down at the ground. When he looked up at me again, he squared his shoulders. "If you ever did decide to leave, to run away, I'd help you. I'd go with you." He stepped toward me again. "I would go with you tonight. Right now."

I was no longer taller than Bird, but I only had to tilt my head up a little bit to look into his eyes. I wanted to see condescension there, mockery.

Instead, there was a depth of caring sincerity that I knew I could trust, if I needed to. That I had always trusted.

"You haven't talked about running away in years," I said. "You used to, all the time . . ." I tried to laugh, hoping he was just trying to lead us toward some other sweet child-hood memory. But the laughter caught in my throat.

"We could live in the woods," he went on, as if talking to himself. "Sure, haven't we spent nearly every free moment up in the trees since we were children? Deep in the forest. John would never find you. No one would ever find either of us." He reached up to undo another of my snarled braids. "We would be happy in the woods, Silvie. You would be free out there."

I felt myself shudder. The ache I felt standing close to his body and saw looking into his eyes was as addictive as warm honey.

"What are you saying?" I whispered.

But my thoughts skittered back to earlier that evening, to the Hunt Ball, to Danton and my brother and my father and all the people to whom I owed my help, my duty, my life.

There was no refuge, no freedom, for me.

"I can't," I said. "I told you. I can't leave them all to him."

The depth and warmth vanished from his eyes; they glinted like mica. "Now *you're* condescending," he said. "Who says we can't get by without you? We common folk. We are tougher, Silvie, than anyone who's been fed and coddled all her life without having to work for it, and you know it, or you're a fool."

My fists clenched. "Yes, Bird, I've been coddled. I've always had food. Delicious food, as much as I can eat, whenever I want it! I've never had to sew my own clothes or patch my own roof, or even feel a chill on a cold day. I've never had to build my own fire. I can ring a bell and get a cup of tea brought to my bed at any hour of the night. And I never—I didn't stand up to my brother. But—" My breath caught. Like Bird, I was afraid I hadn't said what I meant. "But there's still toughness in me, Bird. I know there is."

The kind of toughness I had, that I was *sure* I had, was something I couldn't describe, not even to my best friend. Especially if he didn't see it in me anyway. But by the Lord, I knew it was there.

I felt no longing for him in that moment, and it was a relief. I wanted freedom from that feeling, too.

"I can't run away, Bird," I said. "Maybe I couldn't throttle John in the ballroom, but I can't just abandon everything to him, either, can't just shuck him off and forget. I can't. I don't care if that makes me naive."

He looked at me, biting his lower lip thoughtfully. "You are tough, Silvie. I was wrong to say what I said." He reached toward my face, then lowered his hand to touch my arm instead. "Sure, no one else was brave enough to show that hart mercy today but you."

I smiled sadly at him and took a deep breath. My anger left me just as suddenly as my longing had. "I think . . ." I slipped my hand back into his. "I think I can run away for an hour."

Hand in hand, down toward the river, Bird and I took our solitary way.

❧

Loughsley Abbey sits at the bottom of a huge rockface. It's almost all bare granite all the way to the top, dotted here and there with stubborn heather and gorse. In front of the house is a wide, quiet portion of the North River, which traverses down to our country from Nordsk, breaks into narrow ribbons in the depths of the great forest that separates our manor from Esting City, and then braids together again to make its way to Port End, where our country of Esting meets the sea. Only six months earlier we had seen the sleek, angular explorers' vessel, bound for Port End, that the prince had purchased. In just a few weeks' time Rioch would sail away in search of new lands and—he hoped— new peoples. For our prince was convinced that the proper bride for him waited somewhere not just beyond our own country's borders, but beyond those of any other known country as well.

But I didn't want to think about brides as I walked away from Loughsley and the Hunt Ball and John and Lord Danton waiting inside. I held Bird's hand tighter and walked faster, until we got so close to the edge of the river that I could feel silty water seeping through the soles of my shoes.

The waves made shushing sounds as they touched the

shore and drew back again, touched and drew back. There was a louder, more insistent rushing farther out toward the middle of the river. Clouds had come in and blotted out the moon and stars. Some of the cold had gone out of the breeze.

The air tasted like water and moss, like rot from fallen leaves: deep, earthy, insistent. There were so many layers of perfume and incense and scented oil in the ballroom that even Titan could hardly have discerned the subtler scents from the buffet table, let alone any honest human smells. The air outside was from a whole different world.

I tripped over a rock and bit back a yelp; it seemed wrong to break the whispering quiet of the waterside. Bird caught my arm, then kept walking as though nothing had happened.

We'd left Loughsley Abbey far behind. I looked back; the ballroom's tall windows glowed like gems in the house's East Wing. The word *wing* was apt: the windows' light seemed to lift the house from its rocky cradle, its stand of trees and its vast gardens, all dark except for pinpricks of torchlight. Loughsley looked as if it could take off at any minute, like a bird of prey, and come after me.

Bird and I approached a bend in the riverbank where willow trees trailed their branches like snakes in the dark water. Before us was a covered bridge. A charming, arched confection that my whimsical mother, so I'd always been told, had asked for as a gift from my father, she having so many friends in the village of Woodshire across the river. Even though he disapproved of her friendship with the villagers—as much as my father could disapprove of anything my mother did, which was never much—he had still built it for her. Intricately carved oak and ash made up the path and the roof, showing hearts and flowers and robins in flight, those most commonplace of love symbols. The arch of the bridge was exaggerated, high enough that on the rare sunny day, its reflection in the water made the impression of a perfect circle.

"Do they still call it the Wedding-Ring Bridge, in the village?" I asked.

Bird opened his mouth to answer—I could hear the intake of breath, even though I couldn't make out more than the outlines of his face in the dark—but I put a hand to his chest and stopped him.

My own breath had caught in my throat.

There was someone on the bridge: a tall, bulky figure, hardly visible. I wouldn't have seen it except that the person was not under the deep shadows of the covered walkway at all, but climbing over its side. The figure raised a thick arm to check—what was it, looped around the rail?

I heard a slithering sound as a line suddenly slipped down and cracked straight.

Someone hung by the neck below the bridge, toes just barely touching the water.

# ~THREE~

# *Little Jane*

I ran for the bridge, skidding in my muddy dancing shoes. I wondered, knowing it wasn't what I needed to wonder about right then, whether it would take more time to stop and pull off the useless things or to keep running while they sucked at my feet.

Of the two of us, Bird may have been stronger, but I was still the fleeter. Dancing shoes or no, I reached the bridge before he did.

I could hear gagging, and as soon as I touched the rope I could feel the person on the other end still struggling.

Relief surged through me.

The fall hadn't snapped his neck. It seemed a wonder, given how large and heavy he'd looked from the ground, but I thought someone this desperate deserved at least that small miracle: one more chance that he might not die, not now. Not now.

But for all my archery and riding and the genteel

sportsmanship I prided myself on, I was not nearly strong enough to haul him up again.

Bird was there before I'd finished my thought. "Hold the rope!" he shouted, not at me, but to the person below.

I looked down and saw hands flail upward, blindly groping. Bird wasn't helping me pull, and I couldn't understand it, couldn't think about anything but the horrible gagging noises below us and the splashes of water from his struggling feet.

Finally the hands found the rope and grasped it, heaving upward. The gagging eased, turned to a strangled gasp and then a cough so deep that I could almost feel it racking my body, too.

"Now!" I told Bird. His arms were on either side of mine, tensing hard as he pulled. We leaned back, and I put first one foot and then the other against the rail. Every ounce of my weight, every bit of my strength, went into pulling up the hanging man.

He was pulling himself up now, too; I could feel the rhythmic tugs on the rope, and feel the weight we countered ourselves against coming slowly closer, even before I saw his hands appear between the slats of the bridge.

At that I dropped my feet to the floor again. After a quick glance exchanged with Bird to make sure he wouldn't be surprised, I let go of the rope and leaned over the railing to help the man on the last few inches from suicide.

The hand that grasped mine was broad, sweaty, and even more callused than Bird's. I felt immense strength, and immense weight.

With a few more heaves from Bird and me, he was up over the rail, still gasping and wheezing and coughing that rattling cough. He tumbled over me into the shadows and I tumbled with him, his greater weight pulling me along.

Bird leaned over us and quickly pulled the noose off the man's neck.

We lay gasping together in the pitch-blackness under the bridge's roof, my legs tangled in the man's skirts.

"Thank you," he whispered, his voice as strangled as if the rope still sealed his throat. "I thought . . . I thought . . ."

"Jane," Bird murmured. "Jane, try to breathe slowly."

Jane? I squinted; it was hard to see much in the darkness. Did Bird know . . . her?

The person we'd saved stood up, slowly, and Bird grabbed her arm to help.

She kept standing long after I'd thought she should have stopped, until the top of her head brushed the roof of the bridge, and I could see from the silhouette of her broad shoulders that she was still a little hunched over. The top of Bird's head came up only to her chest, and next to her he looked suddenly small and childlike again.

She was the biggest girl I'd ever seen.

I looked away, embarrassed by how boldly I'd been

staring, and grateful that the shadows had hidden my rudeness. The last thing she needed right now was someone looking at her as if—as if she deserved any scrutiny at all.

"Here," Bird said, bringing his other hand slowly to the small of her back. "Let's get off the bridge."

Jane nodded. Even in the deep darkness I could see her shaking.

Bird guided her down the steep incline and back to the riverbank. I untied the rope and looped it in my arms, then tucked it into the cradle of a tree branch and followed them. I didn't like the feel of it in my hands—it seemed some sticky residue of despair still clung there—and I didn't think Jane would want to look at it again.

In the lesser darkness by the water, I could see a little more of her face, the wide forehead and surprisingly delicate chin, the snub nose, the hard set of her mouth. I could not quite make out the color of her eyes: Green? Gray?

"Silvie," Bird said, "this is Little Jane—ah, Jane Carpenter, daughter of the Woodshire Village carpenter. Jane, this is Lady Silviana of Loughsley." He didn't make the customary bow that was supposed to accompany my title, and I was grateful, but Jane dropped a quick, shaky curtsey that brought her head only a few inches above mine.

"I . . . I know who you are, mistress," she said, still taking strangled, unsteady breaths. "I am more grateful to you than . . ."

I shook my head. "I'm grateful we found you in time," I said, then cringed at my own words. I thought I'd said the wrong thing, but she only nodded and kept looking at the ground.

*More grateful than what?* I found myself wondering. There was a coil inside me, twisting toward some kind of distance from this desperate girl. Snakes in my belly, hissing, chasing each other with wide-open mouths, wanting me to be as different as I could be from this person, from her shaking and misery and despair, so that I would know by our difference that I was well and whole.

I hated myself for it.

Bird touched her arm again, gentle and steady.

Jane didn't move, but even in the darkness I could see her settling under his touch, the way his falcons did, or horses, or me. She felt the same thing those animals and I always felt: that there was a place in him where we could rest.

The question rose silently in the air around us: *Why did you do it?*

I couldn't ask. I was uncomfortable enough with her gratitude. I thought anything I did or said might push her away.

Bird didn't say anything, either. He just stood there, his hand on Jane's arm.

She began to drop. I lurched forward to grab her, but then I realized that she was merely sitting.

Bird looked at me. He pressed Jane's arm lightly, then turned and walked away.

We were left alone in the dark, she and I.

I became too conscious of my own breathing, of the air moving through my mouth and throat. Whispers in the mossy caves inside my chest, breath gathering and releasing in countless tiny spaces; I had seen them illustrated once, the endless forests in the lungs, in one of the huge, dusty books in the library at home. I could just barely see one pinprick of yellow light from the great house far in the distance, or two when the wind made the trees move. I touched my neck, remembering the rope I'd hidden.

I couldn't hear Jane breathing. I saw her falling again, when she was only a faceless shape, and I pictured all the tiny forests in her lungs burning, charring, crumbling into strangled ash inside her body, as if she'd succeeded in what she'd planned to do.

I inched closer to her. I was selfish enough to take at least this one unoffered gift: that I could sit close enough to hear her breathe.

The sounds were steadier now than they'd been even a few minutes before. They might almost have been my own breaths, and that little rasp at the end of the exhale, the hitch when she took in air, might only have been from crying.

Bird's silhouette reappeared. Jagged lines stuck out around his middle, like a child's drawing of a star.

He dropped the pile of lines in front of us, but I couldn't tell what they were. I was still listening carefully, as if Jane's breathing was something I could keep going through the strength of my will.

Bird dug in the pocket of his leather vest, pulled something out, and struck it between his hands. The lines in the darkness resolved themselves into meaning before me as his flint scattered orange sparks around their base. Leaning down, with a few careful breaths, focused and steady, Bird urged the sparks into fire.

The hearth in my room was warm and glowing by the time I woke up every morning. Fire followed me from room to room in Loughsley Abbey: lamps and chandeliers, fireplaces, thick beeswax candles by my bed for reading at night, or by my window for doing nothing but sitting there, watching the quiet river, the endless tumbling wildness of Woodshire Forest beyond it.

But I had never appreciated a fire as I did in that moment, watching Bird coax it into being at the center of the small circle our three bodies made. I had never even bothered to watch one being lit before.

I had a sudden image of a servant waking early, in a dark and cold room, to come to my chamber and stoke the banked coals for me while I still slept, tucked behind the silk brocade drapes surrounding my bed. She'd be a friend of Bird's, perhaps, although not of mine. How many people I didn't know had shared space with me while I slept?

Bird had clearly lit a great many fires before, or maybe this was just a simple skill. I was suddenly embarrassed not to know.

"You can call me Little Jane," the girl murmured suddenly. "It's all right, I don't mind. Even my parents call me that."

Bird bent over the fire again, cupping his hands around the small flame and blowing gently against it, but I saw the rising color in his cheeks. He nodded.

I watched him build the fire, and I felt jealousy curl inside me, jealousy and guilt. Bird was doing something practical that could help this girl, that was helping her already. I watched her wring the water out of her linen skirt, then her cotton underskirt, and spread their hems out in layers by the fire. It wasn't a minute before steam started to rise off them.

She shivered, a kind of relieved shudder. She spread her hands over the fire, flexing and straightening her fingers. I couldn't help but marvel at their size, at the length of the wavering shadows they cast.

What could I say to this girl, who had borne so many more burdens than I had in her life, even though she seemed to be younger than I? What could I say that wouldn't seem condescending, or even cruel?

This girl had tried to die. She had tried to do something that I'd known—even in the greatest depths of misery over my powerlessness in my own family, my own home, my own life—I would never have the hard determination to do.

I shifted a little closer to the fire. I knew I could never kill myself, because . . . because I had wanted to, once, too. I'd wanted to when it had seemed that I had no other way to escape from John's plans for me, from the way he watched me when I climbed trees. I'd wanted to climb so high that he'd never see me again, and if I couldn't do that, to jump . . .

But I'd known at once that I couldn't. Jump.

Little Jane had found that she could. But that didn't mean I didn't know how she felt.

I raised my hands over the fire to warm them, as she was doing.

With both our hands casting long-fingered shadows on the ground around us, we looked like witches at conjuring time. I smiled at the flickering shapes we made, and when I looked at Little Jane again I saw a tiny bit of amusement in her eyes, too.

"Do you need a place to stay tonight?" I asked, suddenly knowing what to say just as surely as I felt I knew what her answer would be—but feeling more than anything that what was most important was asking her what she wanted, rather than telling her I felt I knew it.

The spark of witchy humor I'd seen in her eyes closed in on itself; she shook her head. "No. I mean . . . I won't go home. But I don't want to . . . be a burden."

Bird leaned back from the fire at last, satisfied that it would go on burning without his constant oversight. He looked from one of us to the other. "Surely there's some-where for her to stay at Loughsley," he said. "Some empty servant's quarters."

We both knew how many people John had dismissed, now that my father wouldn't notice.

Jane stiffened. "I couldn't. I couldn't sleep there."

She seemed so certain that I didn't feel I could argue.

Firelight made the open space around us seem smaller, not larger; we were closed together inside a radiant circle. Bird's forehead and cheeks and hair glowed; Little Jane's face, as she shifted her feet closer to the fire and leaned back from it, was cast in shadow. One hand supported her; the other lay across her belly in a manner that tried to seem careless but was not.

That hand across her stomach left a curving shadow.

Suddenly I knew the answer to the question neither Bird nor I had asked, the question that had hissed in the air ever since we'd seen her at the bridge.

She was a tall girl, breathtakingly tall, and broad and wide and thickly set besides: every line of her body was a solid, hulking curve. But the curve of her belly, with the shadow of her hand falling across it . . .

I could tell that Bird had seen it too: not from a change in his movement or a look between us, but from something that had shifted in our little closed circle of light.

Now I was more at ease than he.

I looked at Little Jane again. I no longer saw someone different from me, someone who had grown up in such poorer circumstances that our lives were entirely alien to each other. I saw another young woman, one to whom something had happened that haunted the dreams of every girl, dreams both good and bad. I saw a sister; I saw myself.

"How far along are you?" I asked.

She nodded, her eyes briefly closing. "Five months now," she said. "I've felt her moving for a long time, but my belly only really changed these last few weeks. I managed to keep her hidden for a good while. I thought, maybe . . ." She trailed off.

I knew enough not to speak.

Little Jane kept staring into the fire.

She reached behind her and brought a crooked stick into the circle of light, lightly furred along one side with moss, studded with little pale mushrooms. She tucked it carefully on top of the tallest flame. It grumbled and hissed out steam, and I watched the mushrooms shrivel, the moss grow crisp and brown.

At last the stick cracked and caught. The fire grew to twice its previous height in moments.

Little Jane sighed. "I was hoping I might be . . . that with my size . . . that it might not show at all, until she really got here. That maybe my parents . . . that they'd have to love her, once she came." She poked the fire again. "My father always says how much he loves babies." She sniffed and turned her head. "But I'm not quite big enough to hide her forever." She dropped the stick and rested her hand on her stomach again. "First time I've ever been too small for something. Little Jane." She smiled when she said the name, and the smile was just like the one I'd seen on Bird's face the first time he'd punched John back.

Well, it had been the only time, and Bird had paid for it both swiftly and painfully. But the triumph of the moment, of the smile, was the same.

I'd been thinking of her, carefully, as only Jane, but that rebel smile burrowed into my heart and stayed there. Little Jane.

"When I saw that I couldn't keep her hidden anymore —certainly not in a cottage with only the one room—I knew I had to tell them. And my father, since he's always loved babies, and never thought . . . never thought I'd get married to have one, I told him first. I was fool enough to think he might be happy.

"'Who'd you ride to get that way?' he said," she whispered, her voice going deeper to mimic her father's. "He didn't yell, which was the other thing I'd readied myself for. I thought I could handle getting yelled at. But he hissed it at me, cold and soft."

I tried to imagine how my own father would react if I went to him with such news. With my child, his grandchild, growing inside me.

My father thought the world of me—of both his children. I knew exactly how it would go: first he would ask me if I was all right, or if the pregnancy was hurting me. He'd call for a midwife to make sure of my health.

And then he would ask if someone had done this to me without my consent. If they had, I would know beyond doubt that I'd never see that person again . . . nor, knowing my father, would anyone else.

But if I had "strayed," as my governess used to say abstractly, before I learned what that really meant from the rough talk of John and his friends, and the more natural instruction that no child who spent much time with animals could avoid seeing . . . if I had been with a man, he would still have wanted to help me. I was sure of that much.

At least, that was how he would have reacted before he

fell ill. If I went to him with that news today, he might not even remember who I was.

And John . . . I couldn't imagine what he would do. I didn't want to.

Jane told the rest of her story piecemeal. She didn't cry, or even raise her voice; every few sentences she would simply pause for a long while, looking away from the fire, and then she would stare into its light again and go on.

"I tried to tell him that . . ." A breath. "That I hadn't done that with anyone, not of my own choice, anyway. That I'd been . . . that I'd been forced.

"He leaned back in his chair then, my father, and he . . . laughed at me. He clutched his chest with his big hands.

"'Sure it must have been a great bear, to force such a one as you!' he said when he stopped laughing enough to get the words out." A breath. "I knew it wouldn't do any good to tell him who it was."

Jane looked at me, the first time she'd done so since she'd started talking. "No man would be big enough to force someone my size, of course," she said. "He didn't even have to say so; we both knew it." Another breath. "And it's true. I'm big enough, strong enough. I could fight off anyone. I should have." Two breaths.

I moved my hand slowly, touching her as lightly as I could on the hem of one sleeve. I looked into her eyes, trying to tell her what I knew it would do no good to say.

The forest shrank and grew around us with the pulse of her breathing.

"Anyway, what he did say was no man would bother to force me anyway. I'm not pretty, I know. So I had to be lying, and I had to be a slut. He turned me out of the house before my mother came in from milking."

❧ ❧ ❧

I crept through the halls of Loughsley. I'd brought a candle with me, but I didn't dare to light it with guests of the Hunt Ball occupying so many of our bedrooms. Most of them were likely asleep by then, but I couldn't be sure; and so I moved silently through the darkened halls and stairways, bruising my hips twice when I ran into a table and a banister that I had forgotten. I walked through the house where I'd lived all my life, and it felt as foreign and unknown as a pathless forest.

I did stop, once, before Lord Danton's door. I remembered how he had looked at me when John had accepted his proposal on my behalf. So gentle, so mild. I remembered the deference with which he had bowed to me. He was not a frightening man, not cold or cruel.

I could have a good life with him, I knew, better than many I might have. I could enjoy his offer of "an equal say in the running of things." As Lady Danton I would be mistress of a small estate in the sunny domains near our far-off southeastern border.

I remembered his kind face, his eyes with only the suggestion of wrinkles at their corners, the forty-year-old man who might be my husband, and I nearly stopped at the door and went no farther.

And I remembered John watching both of us, contemplating us as if we were pawns on a chessboard, a small smile on his lips.

"The sheriff has even offered to have us winter here, every year," Danton had told me. I heard someone behind me sigh a little at the generosity of this gift.

But my brother hadn't given this minor lord an offer. It was an order. Once I married, I'd have no claim to Loughsley at all, no way to help anyone who lived here—and in winter I would return, and return, and return, and John would be here. Waiting. Wanting. Giving me to this man was just another way for him to keep me.

Still, a life of security and warmth as a nobleman's wife, and at least my summers spent far away from the nameless fear that haunted me at Loughsley—could I ever hope for more than that?

I was tempted even then to walk into Lord Danton's room, wake him from what I was sure was a gentle slumber, and tell him I was happy for the bargain he and John had made. I could have sealed my fate in that moment.

Perhaps I did.

I turned away from the door and ran outside.

Bird was waiting for me in the secret chair, reclining against its stone back in a way that at first reminded me of a king holding court. But Bird wasn't surveying his subjects or his kingdom. He was looking up at the sky.

There were still the specks and swirls of star and cloud, the smooth coin of the moon sliced by the shifting branches overhead. It was the same sky that had been there all night, but I knew Bird. He could look up into it forever, as if he were a fisherman trying to fathom the depths of the sea.

"Is she all right?" I asked as I approached.

He nodded, still looking skyward. "Asleep in the stables, with a warm drink in her belly. She drifted off all right once she knew I wasn't going to listen to her talk of not being a burden. But she wouldn't even set foot inside the house itself. It seemed to terrify her."

"I know," I said, remembering the look on her face when he'd first suggested she sleep in one of the servants' rooms. "I hate that it scares her so. What is the point of Loughsley, of the house, of my family, if not to protect our people?"

Bird laughed harshly. "The point," he said, "has nothing to do with protection, Silvie, and you know it. The point is what your family takes, not what it gives."

I was ready to slap him. "And what am I trying to do, Bird?" I lifted the stack of warm clothes for Little Jane that I'd taken from my room. "Am I not giving what I can?"

He looked at me then, apologetic, and raised his hands in surrender. But I knew that he wasn't wrong, and I knew, too, that I wasn't giving even a fraction of what I could.

I clutched the clothes tighter. "Jane can't stay in the stables like an animal. And if John were to find her . . ." The nameless fear reared up in me. I swallowed and stopped talking.

Bird looked at me piercingly.

My next words rushed out before I even knew what I was going to say. "And, Bird, I can't stay, either. Not anymore. I want to go to the woods with you, and I want to take Little Jane with us."

## ～ FOUR ～

# *First Night*

**B**ird nodded, standing, and took my hand. "Let's go," he said quickly, as if he were afraid I'd change my mind.

But he didn't lead me away from the estate. Instead, we walked back across the courtyard, and, with the help of a ring of keys I rarely used but always made sure to keep with me, into the storerooms of Loughsley Abbey's gargantuan kitchens.

I hadn't thought, but I was grateful that Bird had.

I readily took a waxed wheel of hard cheese, heavy in my arms, and passed it to him, and I pulled out a barrel of apples and started shoving them into one of the neatly folded flour sacks stacked by the cavelike ovens. But I hesitated in front of the previous day's bread.

"It's your food," Bird said, heaving the cheese wheel onto his shoulder.

"Not this," I said. "Cook used to give the day-old bread to the hens, but I . . ." My cheeks burned; I hadn't wanted

Bird to know at the time, and I still didn't. He tended to roll his eyes at nobles' small acts of charity. "The last day's bread goes to people in the village now, people who need it."

"Old bread's good enough for poor people, I suppose," he said drily.

I whirled on him. "It wouldn't be missed! Do you think I'd be allowed to give away anything that would? Do you think John would allow new bread to go anywhere but our own table?"

Bird shrugged. "True."

I started grabbing loaf after loaf, stacking them until I couldn't balance any more in my arms. "I'm coming, Bird. I'm coming with you. I'm helping Little Jane, or at least I'm trying to. I'm—I tried to stay at Loughsley till now even though it was killing me, even when it killed me every day, because I thought life might be better for the others here if I could . . . counteract him, somehow. John. And none of that was ever good enough, ever virtuous enough, for you. I'm just a spoiled little coward in your eyes, and don't think I don't know it." I was shaking. "Don't think I don't know this is pity, your helping Little Jane and me. Don't pretend it's anything else."

Bird took a loaf of bread from my arms. "Silvie . . ."

"I'll go pack more clothes for the two of us," I said. "We'll get a . . . a wheelbarrow, I suppose, to carry everything."

He put the bread back on the table. "We can't take a

wheelbarrow," he said. "It'd leave a track. We'll bring only as much as we can carry."

"Then we'll leave the apples, too," I replied, my jaw still tense. "There'll be plenty of wild fruit in the forest, anyway." I snatched a fat bag of salt from a nearby shelf instead. It was small enough to carry, and I knew we would need it if we managed to hunt anything large enough to preserve.

Bird's look of surprised approval just made me angrier. I stalked out of the kitchen, heading for my own chamber.

It was easy to pack for Little Jane: even my day dresses had enough excess fabric in the skirts and adjustable laces in the bodices that it would be simple to let them out to fit her.

But for myself, I hesitated. I ran my hands over a fine dark gold wool dress and a green cloak, and realized I'd practically been picturing myself dressing in leaves and flowers, as if I were a spirit of the forest, or one of the lost children from my nurse's story.

I laughed at myself, and I took the dress and cloak with me, as well as my warmest red flannel underskirts. Their colors would fade soon enough, I supposed, and then I'd be as disguised as I should like. Leaves and flowers would hardly keep me warm in the coming winter.

The thought of winter sent a harsh warning through me. I shivered, even in the warmth of my bedroom.

What on earth was I doing? Why on earth would I leave this place?

I looked back at my empty bed. I thought of Little Jane curled up in the stable, believing herself a burden. I thought of Lord Danton sleeping a few rooms away, of the offer he'd made for me. I thought of John . . .

I yanked open a drawer and packed thick stockings for Little Jane and me. I looked in my vanity mirror one last time, at the long hair falling and frizzing around my face, at the emerald drop earrings almost hidden in the dark blond mass. I took out the earrings and stared at them, wondering how much they'd buy us of what we'd need to survive the winter.

But these earrings had been my mother's. All my jewelry had.

I opened my jewel box and placed them carefully inside, letting my fingers run over the plush velvet and then the shellacked exterior as I closed it again.

I'd taken food and clothes. I refused to let anyone think me more of a thief than that.

The clock chimed for two in the morning as I brought my bag through the gardens. It had been the work of an hour to gather everything I needed to leave my life behind.

‿❧ ❧‿

❧ 59 ❧

The nighttime forest was its own species. No trace of the sun-speckled shadows, the warm light dusty with pollen, that I knew so intimately from my years of daytime climbing with Bird. The lush green layers of moss and ivy and sorrel that covered stones, trunks, and fallen and rotting branches all were lost in darkness.

There wasn't even birdsong. Only silence, and the shuffle of six feet.

When an owl hooted overhead, I flinched.

We were too far away from the Loughsley clock to hear it chiming when three came, but I was sure it must have, and the next hour, too. I thought of asking Bird how long it would be until the sun rose, but I was starting to fear that if I said anything that made me seem too coddled, too naive, he'd tell me we shouldn't be doing this at all.

I was unduly grateful for Little Jane's presence at my side, even though, I kept reminding myself, she had to be much more frightened than I was. Even though, of course, I was doing this for her. Of course I was.

Bird walked just ahead of us, carrying a lantern. It wasn't a comfort. I thought the woods might seem less alien, less unknowable, if only we could move through the darkness instead of apart from it. As we walked farther and farther the notion took me over, until it felt as if hidden beasts and monsters walked with us, just outside the lantern's reach.

"Bird," I said at last, "douse the light." I hoped my voice

sounded strong, that I had betrayed no weakness that might make him think less of me.

He stopped. I could see a question forming on his lips as he turned, but when he looked into my face, and Little Jane's, he nodded. "We're just about there anyway," he said, then lifted the lamp and blew it out.

The darkness was a relief. The beasts I'd imagined just outside the circle of the light vanished; or rather, I became one of them, and we were not monsters at all, but only three more creatures sharing the forest with all the others.

And the forest wasn't silent, as I'd thought; there was no birdsong but the occasional owl, true, but there was a kind of rhythm in the air around us that wasn't quite breeze or creaking branches, but a subtler, sleeping version of both. I would never have heard it if I could still see my next steps clearly in the lantern light.

Beside me Little Jane was breathing a bit heavily. I took her hand. "We'll rest for a while," I said.

She laughed. "Not too long," she said. "If I really rest I'll fall asleep. I feel as if I could stay sleeping until the baby comes."

"You can, out here," I said. "No one will ask anything else of you."

Her next breath had a little hitch in it.

In the dark, in the deep forest, it was easy: I put my arms around her.

She rested her chin on top of my head, the surprising hardness of her round belly pressing against me as we held each other. She smelled like sawdust and river water.

"You know, I think we're here already," Bird said, and I could hear him walking a few paces away. When I turned my head to look, still holding Little Jane, I could see him; my eyes had adjusted to the darkness more quickly than I'd expected.

He came back within a few minutes. "Yes," he said, sounding almost giddy. "We're here."

We followed him into a small clearing, small enough to walk across in ten paces. Huge old oak trees ringed it, each at least twenty feet around at its base. And just like the clearing where we'd met the hart — that seemed so long ago now — this one had a rockface at one side.

There was an opening at the rock's base like a mouth, black as could be.

"The cave," I whispered. "Oh, Bird . . ."

I walked toward it as if I were following a memory. In truth, I was. One summer Bird and I had come here every day, and pretended it was our castle.

Bird lit the lantern again and handed it to me, his eyes smiling.

I had to duck my head at the entrance. Inside, the cave expanded, its ceiling rising steeply. There was a small hole in the roof, and in the daytime it let sunshine in. The cavern went back maybe ten yards, its floor increasingly furred with moss that grew wet under the feet in the last few steps. And at the very back, waiting for us, was something I remembered as if in a dream.

A spring. A little deeper and wider than the large bath in my chambers at Loughsley, its sides slick with moss, the water just warm enough to give off small curls of mineral-scented steam.

I trailed my hand through the still surface and briefly closed my eyes in pleasure. I hadn't felt myself grow cold during our walk, but now that liquid warmth seemed like heaven.

How had I forgotten this place?

"Look, Little Jane," I said, but there was no answer.

I turned around. Bird was already busy building another fire, just at the mouth of the cave. Little Jane was huddled in her cape against the wall between him and me, utterly still, so still that it frightened me until I realized she was asleep again.

Surely that was a good sign, I told myself; that she had relaxed enough to sleep so quickly. Surely it meant she could . . . heal, here.

I joined Bird at the fire, watching him carefully and hoping to learn something. "I can't believe that I forgot."

He sat back from the kindling, the fire leaping between us. "I didn't," he said.

"Thank goodness."

He shook his head. I moved closer to him, but as we leaned together I felt a bone-deep weariness.

"Go to sleep," Bird said. "I'm just making sure the fire'll stay going, and then I'll do the same."

I pulled myself upright. It took more effort than it should have, and all my muscles complained. "Happy to obey," I said, and I walked stiffly over to a spot against the wall not far from Little Jane.

❦

I must have fallen asleep quickly, but I awoke almost immediately, my heart pounding.

A face had leaned over me in the darkness. John, come to take me back to Loughsley.

I had to work hard to convince myself, to convince my body, that my brother was nowhere nearby.

There *was* someone beside me when my eyes finally opened, though.

Not John.

Bird.

I reached for him before I was fully awake.

His hands were on my shoulders; he must have been trying to rouse me. "You're all right, Silvie, you're all right," he kept saying.

It was a few seconds before my breath was even. "I know," I said. "Thank you." I hated that he'd seen me that way, so afraid, so vulnerable; but I was grateful, too.

He shook his head, then let me go and stood, turning back toward the fire. As soon as he did, I felt the grip of the nightmare coming back to me.

"Bird." I wasn't going to let myself think about what I said next. "Will you sleep next to me, when the fire's ready?"

"It's ready," he said. "I was just . . . sitting. Thinking."

"About what?" I asked. "Leaving Loughsley? Your mother?"

He smiled softly. "My mother's tough," he said. "She's been telling me for a long time that I should leave Loughsley, leave her. She's always thought it would be good for me to get work somewhere else. That it would help me let go — or grow up, I guess."

I frowned. "You never told me that." I'd wondered, sometimes, if Bird's mother thought he and I were too close; but she was an inscrutable woman, and of course a servant couldn't tell the daughter of the house not to befriend her son.

Bird shook his head. "Why would I? Come now, Silvie." He stood up and joined me by the cave wall. "You know I'd never leave you."

I did. I'd known it all my life, or at least since I was

five. I had taken it for granted, his coming out here with us, bringing Little Jane and me to the forest. What was Bird giving up, in leaving his life at Loughsley? What else had he never told me?

I was too tired, and too grateful, to ask him then. I shifted and spread out my cloak so we could both lie on it.

He opened his own cloak and drew it over us. His was rougher, but thicker, too; warm from his body, with a faint scent of lanolin. He leaned back and I tucked myself against him, my head in the hollow of his neck and shoulder.

I fell asleep more slowly this time, but also more gently, and I looked up all the time toward the place where I remembered sunlight streaming through the cave's ceiling, on that so-long-ago summer.

Just before I drifted off, I saw it glowing a little gray.

## ~FIVE~

# Little Jane Kills the Boar

A bright shaft of sunlight was lancing down by the time I woke later that morning, and Bird and Little Jane were nowhere in sight. Bird's cloak still covered me, and his fire burned merrily, piled with fresh wood; I knew they couldn't have gone far. Smoke swirled into the air and out through the hole many feet above our heads: a natural chimney.

We'd been right as children. This was a castle.

Including its cold, hard stone. When I stood, my back and limbs ached as if I were an old woman.

The hot spring glinted with reflecting sunlight. The cave was still gloomy and cool, but I could see into its shadowy recesses as I hadn't the night before.

They were far from empty. A small collection of tools sat neatly arranged along one wall: I recognized a mallet and an axe, but there were several others whose names I didn't know. A small, dented cauldron and two shallow, rough clay bowls had their own place nearby. I found two wooden drinking mugs and a kettle inside the cauldron. There were a coil of rope and two old blankets there, too.

I tried to pick up the blankets, but in the damp air of the cave, they'd long since moldered through; they sagged and tore under their own weight as I held them. The rope was furred with moss, and the cauldron was rusty. All of it must have been there for years.

I frowned and replaced the blankets. Limping, still sore, I made my way outside in search of my friends.

Bird emerged into the clearing, carrying more firewood. Seraph perched on his shoulder, grooming herself with her hooked beak. Bird dropped the timber just inside the cave's mouth with a heavy exhale, then turned to me. "Easy as finding wood in a forest," he said with a grin. He chucked Seraph under the chin, and the fearsome bird chirped like a pet canary.

I stretched. "If only it were as easy to find feather beds."

Bird scoffed, mock offended. "I hope you're not suggesting any violence toward my lass, here."

"I would never. And I suppose I did sleep on a Bird, even if he doesn't have feathers."

I said it smiling, but Bird's cheeks reddened a little, and

he looked right at me, suddenly serious. "We should find more bedding, of course," he said quietly. "Were you cold last night, Silvie?"

I shook my head. "Not at all, thanks to you." I paused. "Bird . . . the blankets and tools, inside the cave . . . did you bring them here? Did you know . . ." I hated to think Bird might have known my own mind before I did, might have known me better than I knew myself.

He stepped forward and clasped my arm. "I didn't know, Silvie. I just wanted us to have the choice, the chance, to go to the woods, to be safe here. I'd be surprised if we can even use much of it now, although I'll be glad of the pot to boil our drinking water."

"When?" I could feel how tense my arm was under his hand, but I couldn't make it relax. "When did you stock the cave?"

"Years ago. Years . . . I was ten, I think. I had great faith in myself, thought I could be some kind of hero. John was starting to—" he hitched his breath. "I was thinking of our summer out here, and I wanted to give us that freedom back. Just in case you ever wanted it again. But I never *knew*, Silvie. I never presumed. I just wanted you to have another choice than—what I thought they were going to force on you. Your father, and John."

"My father would never—" I couldn't finish the

sentence. I suddenly wasn't sure at all of what my father would have chosen for me, if his mind were still sound. He had been so orderly and prideful in his prime, pious, strict with the tenants of his estate, a model lord and servant to his crown.

Anyway, what good would it do to wonder what choice I might have had, in some other life? My father's mind had eroded, John was lord and sheriff, and I . . . I ran away. I chose the forest, the freedom my friend had wanted for me.

"Thank you, Bird. For the choice. And for . . . for keeping me warm, out here."

Silence stretched out after my words. Bird just kept looking at me in his grave way. Where his hand lay on my arm, I almost thought I could feel the beat of his heart.

"You're a great man to start a fire," I added brusquely, in the same gruff tone Bird's mother had always used when she praised her son, and in a pale imitation of her rough North Esting accent, too.

Just enough mirth came back to his face that the moment between us was broken and I could relax again. "Starting a fire is one thing," he said. "Keeping it from quenching is much harder. But between the three of us I'd say this fire needn't go out all winter."

I swallowed. The specter of winter made me shiver

again, just as I had when I'd thought about which clothes to bring for myself and Little Jane, back at Loughsley the previous night. I ran away from the idea of it as fast as I could. In my mind we three wandered through a perpetual autumn forest full of red leaves that glowed like Bird's fire, safe and free and unfreezing, forever.

Some brambles nearby echoed the harvest-time image in my mind: heavy with glossy black fruit, their papery copper leaves wound between branches thick with thorns. "I thought I might pick blackberries today, and dry some over the fire," I said. "We might want them . . . later."

I couldn't even quite make myself say the word *winter*. How foolish, how naive, to imagine we could survive out here . . .

*Don't think about it.*

I took a berry and raised it to my lips.

Picking blackberries was one of my few good memories with John. We'd wander the edge of the estate together, down to the bridge and then back home, eating berries all the way, until our mouths were stained with juice — or mine was, at least. John didn't like to eat them himself, but he'd find a particularly big and juicy one, examine it, and then tell me to open my mouth. I'd catch the berry he threw, every single time. I was only little, maybe four or five, but blackberry-picking with my brother was a precious, peaceful memory for me—compared to all my worse memories of him, at least.

Something else I didn't want to think about. I popped the berry into my mouth and lingered over the flavor of the rich, thick juice.

"That's a good idea," Bird said. "I'll help you string them this evening." He started to stack the firewood into a neat pile. "Just watch out for worms, of course."

I had been about to swallow, but his teasing made me laugh, and the end result was a kind of choking cough. I waved him away when he came over to pound my back.

After I caught my breath, I said, "You're not going to fool me so easily again, Bird. We aren't children, and blackberry worms aren't as scary as the dragons you said lived in the damson tree."

"Ah, but I got to eat all the damsons, didn't I?" He smiled and pulled a fat berry from the bramble. "I'm not telling stories, though. Look." He showed me the stem end.

It was white in the middle, between the black globes. I pursed my lips at him as I leaned in ever so slightly to see. I was more than ready for him to squish the berry against my face.

Then it moved.

A translucent, ridged worm sat curled up in the white center. It raised its eyeless head as if looking at me.

I knew at once why John had looked at each blackberry he gave me. Not to check that worms weren't in the ones I ate, but to make sure they were.

I swallowed again, a seed stuck in my throat.

"They're harmless," Bird said quickly. "In fact, a bit of extra meat will do us good, going into winter. That's all they really are." He cupped his hand and lifted the berry to his mouth.

"Don't!" I said, smacking it away.

I was afraid Bird would laugh at me, but he didn't. "We can flick them out as we string them," he said. "They're only in maybe one out of five, mostly."

I didn't want to tell him about John, about my one good memory stolen. Bird already despised my brother, and there was no point in driving that anger deeper. Not now that I was free of him.

But hungry as I was, I ate no more blackberries that day.

❧ ❧

When we'd been in the woods for two weeks, I shot a boar.

I'd climbed a tree a half mile or so from the clearing, just high enough that I could catch the warmth of the thin sunlight that managed to plunge that far through the leaves. I had girded my skirts for the climb, and now I stretched my bare legs in front of me, flexing my ankles and feeling the warmth on my skin, and the gentle breeze over the fine hair on my legs. I'd brought my bow because I carried it always; Bird had won the argument that I needed it for my own safety, but I still told myself I was holding on to it for hunting. The bread and cheese I'd brought from home were carefully rationed every day, and worms or no, blackberries were quickly becoming our staple food. Bird's falcon had to feed herself now, and so far she'd caught only mice and voles, which we hadn't quite persuaded ourselves to eat.

We all missed meat.

I closed my eyes and turned my face up to catch another narrow shaft of sun.

I heard the sounds of the forest all around me: the leaves and branches that shifted and groaned so much like waves that it was almost as if I was back at Loughsley, listening to the lap of water against the rocks and cattails on the shore. Birds cackled and twittered and whooped. The sunlight felt as if it had its own noise, too, as liquid as the watery sound of the leaves. I heard its warmth as a smooth trickle running across my eyes and over my face, down from my knees to my feet.

A heavy whuffling broke my reverie. I stayed as still as I could, opened my eyes, and slowly rolled sideways so that I could see down toward the ground, toward the source of the phlegmy snorting. My legs gripped the branch on either side and I leaned forward, lifting my bow and arrow from my back.

The snuffling creature lumbered into sight: a boar. I was a little disappointed; I'd been hoping for another hart, like the one from the royal hunt. There's more meat on a deer.

But there was still a fortnight's good eating for the three of us in a boar, and a thick hide for warmth besides, if we could figure out how to cure it out here.

I took aim.

I hit the boar just above the heart. But the hide I coveted must have been thick indeed, because I could still see the base of the arrowhead after I struck my mark; I'd barely penetrated the skin.

The boar squealed and whirled around in a circle, trying to crane its huge, blocky head back far enough to see the source of its sudden pain.

I aimed again, this time aiming for its jaw, where any hunter knew that a great vein lay close to the surface. If I could puncture that, the boar would fall in seconds, and die in seconds more.

But the animal was moving fast, and I missed my mark: I struck it in the back of the neck, just missing the spine. It stopped whirling and began to buck and kick at the air with its sharp black hooves. The noises it made now weren't squeals, but screams not unlike those a human could make.

I could smell its panic drifting up to me thicker and thicker, a rank odor like old, sour sweat.

I felt tears in my eyes. I had to bite down on the inside of my cheek, hard, before the pain was enough to steady my hands and pull me back from abject misery over the boar. It had never taken me more than two shots to make a kill before, not even my first time; the huntswoman made well sure that anyone she taught to shoot was able to kill cleanly before they were allowed to try it.

But remembering Bird's mother only made me feel worse. She'd always been kind to me, and I thought of what Bird had told me over the fire, that she'd wanted him to go somewhere new. He hadn't said the real reason, and he hadn't needed to: his mother had seen our friendship, seen the warmth and longing I sometimes felt, and she wanted him to be free of those things. Free of me.

Now that he'd brought me to the forest, he might never be.

All these thoughts filled the space of only half a moment, half a heartbeat, and I set them aside to focus on the boar.

I swallowed the blood in my mouth. I forced my hands to still again as I gripped the third and last arrow I'd brought with me. I breathed in, took aim . . .

And Little Jane appeared in the clearing.

The boar noticed her just a moment before I did, and

it froze—and then it turned on my new friend, shaking its shaggy head and dragging its long, cracked tusks through the air. It reared up, my useless arrows sticking out at strange angles like demon horns.

It brandished its tusks and charged.

"Little Jane, look out!" I yelled, scrambling down the tree, my bow and last arrow still in my left hand.

She didn't move: she stood directly in the path of the beast, staring it down from her great height. Her hands were behind her back, and she didn't even put them out to defend herself.

Then, as the beast charged her she raised both arms over her head so quickly that I could not clearly see what they held, only that it was some long dark shape that she brought down in a blur on the boar's broad skull.

It fell to the ground and lay still. Its head was a split fruit, glistening red.

Jane lifted her staff, a thick branch of witchwood nearly half as tall as she was. Blood dripped off it and trickled down her hands.

I walked toward her, staring, and she smiled. "Couldn't let you leave that job unfinished," she said. "I wanted to eat tonight." She glanced at the multitudes of brambles around us and wrinkled her nose. "*Really* eat."

I nodded. "Me too. Thank you." I crouched down to

examine the boar: its smell was so strong that I had to cover my mouth and nose with my sleeve. It was rutting season, which explained why he'd wandered so boldly close to our camp. It also explained the stink.

Its skull was as thick as my thumb was wide. Even the bone splinters around the crater Little Jane had made in its brain were solid and broad. I tried to imagine what it would be like to wield such force, such strength, as she had in her arms. I couldn't.

"I envy you, Little Jane," I said, pulling my first arrow from where it had lodged above the boar's heart.

I looked up at her, smiling, but her face had gone closed-off again, and she turned away.

❧ ❧

Juice from the heart, liver, and kidneys sizzled and crisped over the fire, turning from pink to red and then deep golden-brown. Bird turned the spit so expertly that not a single drop fell wasted into the coals.

The smell tormented me: rich and sweet, seductive enough to cut through the boar's lingering bloody musk.

Little Jane and I had cleaned the animal where we'd felled it, to save the offal from souring inside its belly, and we'd left the carcass hanging from a tree to drain. It was high enough to be safe from bears, and far enough from camp that we hoped it wouldn't draw them to us, either. I'd scrubbed my arms of blood in a nearby stream, and Little Jane had plunged in altogether, shrieking at the cold. I'd shared my dry clothes with her and used her blood-spattered overdress to carefully wrap the offal.

Seraph picked at the intestines, which we'd packed at the bottom of our makeshift sack; the waste inside meant we could not eat them ourselves.

But the heart of a wild beast was prized meat for any hunter.

As the boar's dispatcher, Little Jane had the honor of eating it. Bird presented it to her with the same flourishing bow that I'd seen his mother use after the culmination of so many hunts.

She shook her head. "Give the heart to Lady Loughsley," she said, nodding toward me. "The boar was her quarry to begin with."

I pulled away, though I was impatient and hungry. "You made the kill, Little Jane," I said. "The heart's yours."

Little Jane bowed her head. "You should have it in truth, my lady. You're the mistress, our leader out here, same as at home."

I resisted the urge to laugh. I'd shown time and again that I was the least knowledgeable, the least helpful, of our group. Of the three of us, I knew well that I was the only one who wouldn't have survived that first night in the forest alone, even with all my pretenses to plant knowledge and hunting skills.

I couldn't even start a fire. I depended on my two companions for everything.

I looked to Bird, expecting him to say as much, to add something about how spoiled and helpless I was, but he was silent. After a moment he turned toward me and, although with only a nod instead of the full bow, he offered the dripping heart.

The scent of its smoky sweetness drifted over me, and my mouth flooded.

I took the meat from Bird. It was still hot enough from the fire that my fingers started to throb.

"We'll share it," I said. "Eating a heart is meant to give you courage, isn't it? We all need as much of that as we can get." I glanced at Little Jane. "I'd say the baby does, too. But I will accept this heart from you only as a gift, and not as my due." I realized I was speaking officiously, and felt suddenly embarrassed. "Is that all right?"

Little Jane looked at me wryly. "As you wish, mistress," she said. Out of the corner of my eye I saw Bird grin, but whether it was at what I'd just said or what he knew I was about to say next, I couldn't guess.

"Please, as—as one more gift," I said, "just call me Silvie. I'm mistress of nothing out here."

I lifted the heart to my mouth and took the first bite.

My whole body sang with the relief of nourishment, so that I felt as if I could taste it in my whole body, right down to my toes.

I heard a growl and realized that it came from me: my throat was rumbling as if I were a beast of prey.

I silenced myself with surprising difficulty as I swallowed. I offered the meat to my friends, smiling, the juices still on my lips.

Little Jane shook her head, but she consented to eat her share of the heart.

## ~SIX~

# A New Home

It seemed like a miracle when the light woke me up the next morning, not a cramped and empty belly. I lifted Bird's arm from my shoulder. He smiled in his sleep and flexed his fingers.

Little Jane was already awake, warming her hands by the fire at the mouth of the cave.

"Someday I'll be up before both of you," I said, "I swear . . ." But a yawn overtook my last words, and Little Jane laughed.

"Sure you're used to sleeping in, Lady—Silvie," she said. "You don't have to change everything about yourself right away, you know."

There was something about that statement I didn't much like, but she went on before I could parse it. Leaning back with her hands resting on her hips, she surveyed the huge oak and pine branches above us.

"None of us are sleeping well on the ground, anyway," she murmured, as if to herself, "least of all me, to be frank.

I can feel her at night, shifting around, and then I have to shift around, too. It's hard enough to fall asleep there, and what's cold and hard now will only get colder and harder as the season turns." She cleared her throat; the coming winter was on all our minds, but none of us liked to talk about it.

"Oh, Little Jane, I didn't realize . . ." Every time I thought I'd seen all the facets of my selfishness, something new confronted me.

She tutted. "Why would you? Not your job to think of such things. I copped it the first night, of course, but one of the things I do know about having babies is that I shouldn't carry around too many heavy things. I'd've started cutting the first day, otherwise."

I straightened and came blinking out of the cave. I bent down to touch my toes, and when I stood up, Little Jane was giving me one of her skeptical, surveying looks. "I know you've never hewn wood before, but I don't suppose you'd mind learning, if it meant we could sleep in a tree house—off the ground?" She nodded back into the cave.

I shivered, then nodded enthusiastically. "I'd do more than that for a warm, dry floor," I said. "And . . . I hate to say it, but . . ."

"But the cave feels like a trap," Little Jane said quietly. "I know. Only one way in and out. It's been giving me nightmares, too."

"I haven't—" I stopped myself. Sleeping with Bird

helped ease my dreams, but they were still there: shadowy faces leaning over me as I slept, small rooms, tight spaces, binding bedclothes. The freedom that I'd so longed for could seem very far away in the cave at night.

"You're right," I told Little Jane. "It is a trap. If anyone found us there — say, highwaymen" — I refused to think of John — "we'd be served up on a plate. But sleeping in the trees, we'd always have the upper hand. We'd hear them coming, and we could be gone before they'd begun to climb." I felt as if I were planning a war strategy, and I told myself that was foolish. It was only us three runaways out here, after all, not an army.

But the life that we were somehow eking out together was worth a little planning, a little protection. Warlike or not, I would guard it if I could.

I nodded at Little Jane.

"Good," she replied. "If we get started today, the wood should be just about dry enough to build with before too many hard frosts, if we're lucky. Not that we'll have much of a choice." She paused and chewed on a thumbnail. "It'd take forever to get these trunks hewn. Might be impossible, really. Of course, we might not want to make it as clear as a tree stump where we're staying anyway, right?"

I looked up into the trees along with her. "Surely there are some fallen trees we could chop up for wood?"

"They'd be rotten," Bird said, rubbing his hands over

his face as he came out of the cave and joined us. "Ground's damp, remember?"

"I've been sleeping on it this past week, too," I answered. He had that Silvie's-not-thinking tone in his voice again, the one that set my teeth on edge.

But then I remembered how he'd put his arm over me when I'd shivered the night before, so obviously not wanting to take anything with his touch, only to give. Maybe all the practical knowledge I lacked annoyed him, but *I* didn't. The understanding that Bird loved me, in his sometimes curmudgeonly way, was always there, always clear. I held on to it then, when I wanted to snap at him again.

"If they were freshly fallen, they'd have cured a little but not had time to rot," I said, keeping my voice even. "Although I suppose even then"—I looked back at Little Jane, who still gazed up toward the canopy—"it would be too conspicuous to clear out whole trees, even fallen ones."

"Aye," she said, still distracted. "We'll cut down branches. Big ones, but high enough up that they won't be obvious. We'll have a small and oddly shaped little tree house, but at least it'll be warmer and drier than the cave. And—and safer."

I smiled at her, not wanting to dwell on our shared fears. "Right now, I can't imagine anything better."

An hour later I found myself up in a tree with Bird again, each of us holding on to one handle of a saw and pulling it back and forth across the base of a branch that was at least three feet thick.

My shoulders had gone past aching, and then burning, into a sort of helpless numbness. The canopy was too dense to see the position of the sun in the sky, and I had to admit that even if I'd been able to see the sun I wouldn't be able to read the time with much accuracy. All I could do was push, pull, and not think about how many more times I'd have to do it.

"Boar again tonight?" I called across to Bird over the persistent wheezing of the saw.

"Aye," he said. "Lady and Lord, I could eat the whole beast myself."

I thought with trepidation of our stores for winter, but with my head growing light from hard work and hunger, I couldn't disagree.

"Hold!" Little Jane yelled. The branch between us creaked, a low whine that I could feel vibrating through the tree itself, out through my legs and up my torso.

It was harder than I expected to force my arms to stop moving. As soon as I did, it was as if I'd given them permission to tell me how much pain they were in. The muscles in my shoulders immediately seized up.

With a ghostly moan, the tender skimmed-milk green

wood underneath the thick bark revealed itself and the bough peeled slowly away. The wood cracked and leaves fluttered delicately as the huge branch fell.

With great effort and pain, I managed to get down to the ground again. Sweat cooling on my face, I turned to smile at Little Jane.

"No more sleeping in that cave," I said through my heaving breaths.

She raised an eyebrow. "No indeed. In a few months, we'll have wooden floors."

I could only stare.

❧ ❧

There is a special kind of moss that grows on evergreen trees in Woodshire Forest. Thick, springy, and dense, sheep's moss is best known for becoming both softer and stronger as it dries. While Bird and I finished cutting and splitting wood, Little Jane spent the rest of that day gathering the moss, using a small knife from Bird's stores to pare long strips from the rough, rucked bark of the pines and firs. She'd been gathering it since our first day in the forest, piece by piece; in another week or so she would have enough for us to replace the makeshift, scratchy leaf beds we'd made after that first night.

When she returned in the evening, craning her neck to see over the armful of moss she carried, Bird was turning a cut of boar on the spit. The rest of the animal hung from the roof of the cave, near the opening so that it would catch the rising smoke. Between the smoke and the salt—we'd rubbed nearly the whole precious bag of salt we'd brought from Loughsley's kitchens into the meat—we could only hope we'd done enough to preserve our quarry.

I was watching Bird carefully, trying to memorize his technique. "You really need to let me cook sometime," I said.

"You really need to learn how first," Bird replied mildly. "If you think I'm going to risk wasting any of this, you're very wrong. You women stick to hunting, and I'll tend the hearth."

"Ah." I set down the chamomile I was stringing to dry along with the blackberries. Before I stumbled across the boar—or it across me—I'd spent my first days in the forest gathering edible plants. It was the only knowledge I had that my friends lacked, and I felt sharply grateful that I could contribute something of my own. "I hunted these down yesterday, too." I held up three large cattail roots from a marshy spot I'd stumbled on near one of the streams. "I don't think they'll taste very good, but they're safe to eat, at least. And they don't die in the winter, so before the ground freezes hard we can dig up lots more."

Bird stared at the misshapen brown bulbs. "That's wonderful, Silvie. That's perfect."

"We just have to stab them before we put them in the coals," I muttered, taking out the knife I'd started keeping in a sheath at my side to do just that. "Otherwise they explode." If I couldn't cook, I was determined that my small knowledge of plants would be useful, at least.

And the tubers, it turned out, were delicious.

❧ ❧

We'd been in the forest a fortnight when Little Jane started getting sick.

It was only small things at first, signs she tried her best to hide from us: paleness when she stood for too long; eyes that didn't seem to focus at the end of the day; the way she often had to lean against a tree trunk, and then to sit with her hands supporting her head, while she told us how to hew the timber. It had become clear that she was right about how long building would take—we'd be lucky to have our tree house up by the new year.

I could have faced a winter in the cave, however reluctantly. Baths in the hot spring were a favorite ritual, and Bird's fire had never yet gone out. Seraph started to bring in rabbits and even the occasional trout. I could nearly forget the trapped feeling in the cave, most nights, with Bird's arm around me, his steady sleeping breath in my ear. But for Little Jane's sake, as each week wore on and her belly grew while the rest of her seemed to fade . . . She couldn't go on like that. And I wouldn't let her.

"You should go in to see the Mae," Bird said one evening as we sat around the fire, when Little Jane had set down her portion of tubers and boar without eating. "Little Jane, please. You're not well."

She shook her head. "I can't go back there," she said, "to the village. I never want to — to see them ever again." She stared into the flames. "I know what they must think of me, now that I've left. Since my family hasn't kept me, and I haven't kept my honor. I know they all think the way my father does."

I felt my heartbeat quicken with anger. "Kept your honor? Died, you mean?"

Little Jane still looked at the fire. "You went to church growing up same as I did, Silvie, even if your church was prettier. You know the saints same as I do."

I swallowed. I understood precisely what she meant: Every story of a female saint ended the same way. The girl chose to die rather than to live in dishonor, whether that meant marrying a heretic or disavowing the faith . . . or submitting to rape. Her death was what made her a saint.

"Surely there's more honor in — in going on," I said. "Surely that's what we're doing out here. We're making our own honor, instead of letting other people tell us what it means."

The truth was, I was more certain of Little Jane's virtue than my own, surer that she deserved protection and freedom. Believing that she needed those things was my excuse to give them to myself, too. But if she didn't know that already, I wasn't going to say it out loud.

"I know," Little Jane said. "But even so, I can't bear to think of how they'll look at me back home. I'm going on, I *am*. I'm here, aren't I? But I'll do my going on *away*."

I was still almost shaking with anger, that Little Jane should feel that way, that the people she'd grown up with should *make* her feel it. But Bird's voice, when he spoke again, was as calm as the water in the spring behind us.

"The Mae is a woman of the church, Little Jane, and I don't think she would call you dishonored."

Little Jane laughed softly. "Maybe not. She's always had her own funny notions. But it's not her I want to avoid."

I had an idea. "Where does the Mae live?"

"The parsonage annex," Bird said, "at the edge of the village."

"What if we went at night, then? What if we went to her when the rest of the village was sleeping?"

Little Jane looked hopeful for a moment, but then she shook her head again. "I wouldn't want to be a bother," she muttered.

This time it was Bird who started to get angry. "Lady and Lord, Jane, you're not—"

I caught his eye, and he stopped.

"Surely it would bother her more, a midwife as she is, if something happened to you out here that she could have helped to prevent," he finished.

Jane's jaw clenched. "I suppose so."

"Right, then." I bit into my tuber with gusto. "We're going tonight." A Sistren midwife with "her own funny notions"—even without Little Jane's clear need, this was someone I wanted to meet.

# ~ SEVEN ~

## Mae Tuck

L ady and Lord, Silvie, it's just a few tea leaves."

"And a sack of oats. Or two. And maybe some more apples."

"Sure, why not?" Bird bent down to pick a sprig of mint, then placed it in his mouth. "It's only as much as you'd eat if you were still here. It's not robbery."

"But I'm *not* here." I pulled my hood low over my forehead. It was night, and the heavy cloak and men's trousers I'd borrowed from Bird kept me disguised, but I didn't want to take chances. The feeling that John's eyes were on me had grown stronger as we'd left the forest and approached Woodshire Village. When Little Jane had parted with us to go see the midwife, and Bird and I had crossed the Wedding-Ring Bridge and made our way back to the gardens at Loughsley, that queasy feeling had only grown stronger.

I tucked more peppermint into my pockets. "Isn't it enough that I helped Little Jane get away, Bird—and, Lord, that I left myself? Do I really have to steal food from my own family, too?" I clenched my fists, sticky with mint sap. "How much more are you going to ask of me?"

"*I* ask of *you?*" Bird's eyes flashed. "Has it even occurred to you, Silvie, what I've given up to bring you and Little Jane to the forest?"

"You asked me to come! You begged me."

He froze, every line of his body stiff. He stalked away toward the secret chair.

I followed him quickly, already ashamed of what I'd just said. I hadn't thought—or rather, I'd pushed the thoughts away. I remembered feeling that I'd betrayed Bird's mother by not killing the boar cleanly. I'd known even then that I'd betrayed her far more deeply by taking her son away.

Bird stood facing the chair, staring at it.

I sat down, then looked at him pleadingly.

"You gave up your whole life for me—for Little Jane and me, I mean. I know that, Bird. I'm so grateful to you that it's hard for me to think about it. That I *don't* think about it. But I should. You gave up your family, your work, your income, your place in the community . . . you gave up everything. For me, for Little Jane. And I've never even thanked you."

His shoulders dropped, and his stance relaxed. After a moment he joined me on the chair. I kept looking at him, trying to tell him with that look that I was sincere.

Finally he embraced me, cupping the back of my head

and bringing it to rest on his shoulder. "I did ask you to leave," he said. "I won't say beg, but I asked so many times . . . You saw the supplies I had ready in the cave." I could feel his fingers slowly stroking the wool of my hood. "I've always seen the wrongs here, the injustices. When John beat us, I knew as well as you did we could never tell anyone. John would never be held accountable, nor would his friends, as long as they had money or his protection. I never even told my mother — just said I'd hurt myself playing, climbing trees."

I pictured Bird's sharp-eyed, skeptical mother. "She must have seen through that."

He shrugged. "Probably. Well, definitely. But didn't she know the same thing? Doesn't she spend her life guiding rich idiots through the hunts, protecting them, finishing the kills they can't make themselves, and all for barely enough pay to keep the two of us alive? She never was invited to the Hunt Balls, Silvie, not even in your father's prime. The huntswoman." He took a shaky breath, and it was obvious that the slights against his mother bothered him more than those against himself. "So, no, I don't feel I've given much up in leaving my work behind. We still hunt in the forest, don't we? But now the lass and I get to keep all our kills, and share them only with those we love, those who need them. Not give them in tax to rich bullies like your brother, to be left hungry ourselves."

I heard a rustle of feathers; Bird's falcon was never far away.

"But you left *her*, Bird. You left your mother. And your friends—sweethearts, I don't know—in the village. Everyone you love."

"Perhaps." Bird lifted his hand for Seraph to catch as she landed, and I looked up. The falcon had something tied to her right foot: a rolled piece of paper. I realized it must be from his mother.

"We have our ways of staying in touch, she and I. It's useful, too, to know what goes on back here—to know if John starts sending out search parties, for instance."

I flinched. That was something else I hadn't let myself think of.

Bird stroked Seraph's back. She pressed herself briefly up against his hand, then took flight again. Bird tucked the paper into his vest pocket.

We watched her climb the sky. "I wish I could do that," he said. "See everything from above so clearly, as she does. As the Lady and Lord must do." He paused with a chagrined half-smile; Bird had always been more religious than I was, and we'd had our share of spirited arguments about each other's beliefs.

Just then, though, I found myself wishing for the same divine clarity Bird sought. I nodded, briefly closing my eyes before I reopened them to the ocean of stars.

"Sometimes I think I'd know how to fix the world, if I could only see it from far enough away. Going to the woods with you feels a bit like that. And as for everyone I love . . ." He looked away from the night sky and toward me. "Well, Silvie. You know all about that."

I felt a glow steal into my skin. I touched Bird's cheek, but that wasn't enough. I embraced him as he had me, pulling his head to my shoulder. "I love you too, Bird."

We kept perfectly still against each other. I hardly wanted to breathe; there was something both holy and fragile between us just then. Almost holy enough to make me believe.

I made myself take that breath. I pulled away from Bird, gently, knowing what I had to do next. "I don't want to steal from Loughsley, but . . . you're right. I'm entitled to a few tea leaves . . ." Bird began to smile in earnest, and I grinned right back at him. "And a couple bags of oats. We still have some time before we're due to meet Little Jane."

❧ ❧

Bird was waiting when I got back to the stone chair. I set down the sack of staples I'd brought from Loughsley's kitchens: tea leaves, salt, dried beans, a small and precious bag of sugar. Bird had oats and barley from the stables.

Little Jane wasn't with him.

"She's gone back to the cave already?" I asked, hopeful

but doubting. I adjusted the hood that kept my face shadowed. It was hot, especially with my long hair wound up under it, but I wouldn't take it off, or the thick scarf that concealed my mouth, until we were deep in the woods again. "To rest?"

Bird shook his head. "Not back yet."

Suddenly the nebulous sicknesses and fears I'd faced in my old home began to seem trivial and foolish. The only reason Little Jane wouldn't have appeared would be if there was something wrong with her, with the pregnancy, something that worried the much-admired Mae Tuck enough to keep her there long past our planned meeting time.

"Right," I said. "We have to go to her."

"We have to get out of here before dawn," Bird said, "get all of this back to the cave, and cover our tracks, too. We won't do Little Jane much good if your sheriff brother finds us, or if we starve to death this winter."

"Bird—" I wanted to tell him that he wasn't being fair, always assuming I'd forgotten the practical things. "Just because I don't always think of the same things first that you do, that doesn't mean that I want us to starve."

Bird glared at me. "*Want* us to? Of course not, but how do you think we'll keep that from happening? Not by holding each other's hands, Silvie. We live by food and warmth and shelter now, or at least, we live by those things before we get the luxury of thinking of anything else. Kind intentions are no good without bread."

I remembered the warm embrace in which we'd woken up that morning, and the one we'd shared just a few hours ago. In the coming winter it wouldn't be enough, I knew that, but still . . . still, that closeness didn't have to be nothing.

"If Little Jane needs us, that's more important," I said. "We can always come back for food later. This is still my— These things are—" I couldn't quite say *mine,* or *home,* either. Just knowing John was close by made me feel sick.

But Little Jane . . . she had endured something the likes of which I, feeling sick over a brother who sometimes looked at me in a way I didn't like to think about, couldn't even imagine. And all she wanted, and all that I could give her, was love and kindness, freedom in the wake of horror. That was a kind of warmth, a kind of food, even if Bird couldn't see it.

"I'm going to get her," I told him in the Daughter of the House voice he hated, the imperious tone with which I'd first asked him why he knew my name. "Do what you like with the food."

I stalked off through the woods and down toward the river and the Wedding-Ring Bridge, but after a few steps I had to turn around. I could feel my face flaming as I said to Bird, "If you will only tell me where Mae Tuck lives."

"I'll show you," he said, and I was grateful that he didn't laugh.

∽∘ ∘∽

Mae Tuck's annex, it turned out, would have been easy to miss.

Whitewashed, with a freshly thatched roof that was barely taller than I was, it hardly seemed like the grand accommodations most clergy had. Brother Mayhew, who had overseen the spiritual life of the village since before I was born and who was a good friend of my father's, lived in the main house. That was made of stone, tall and spacious and well-appointed.

This outbuilding, in comparison, might as well have been a shed. I was sure that Little Jane couldn't stand up straight inside it.

I was so taken aback by how small the place was that it took me a few minutes to realize that no smoke was rising from the chimney, and that no light, not even a candle, burned inside.

I knocked cautiously on the door. There was no answer.

Someone moaned behind us.

I whirled around.

There, sitting on the ground huddled against the parsonage's garden gate, was Little Jane.

"I only felt weak when I came," she said. "But when I found she wasn't here, I got dizzy, I . . . I just had to sit down for a while. I think I'm . . . sicker than I realized." She touched a hand to her forehead; the motion was so feeble it made my heart ache. "You were right to tell me to come here."

I crouched and took her hand. "Is the baby . . ." I wasn't sure what to say.

"Oh, she's grand. Getting stronger every day, only . . . it's as if she takes it from me. She'll probably be bigger than I am by the time she comes out." Little Jane tried to smile at her joke, and so did I. Neither of us succeeded.

"Look," Bird whispered. He pulled down a piece of paper that had been hammered into the frame of the window near the door.

*Taken to Woodshire Jail,* it read, *for grievous offenses against the noble family of this village.*

"John," I whispered.

❧ ❧

I'd never been to the jail before. I hadn't even thought about it much, only been glad that it was there, to keep us safe from the brigands and thieves and highwaymen whom John always bragged about capturing.

"It's so . . . small," I murmured. Not just small: the stone building was squat and dilapidated. It looked neglected, too: the walls had been whitewashed once, but only a few worn patches remained, and parts of the heavy timber door were pocked with woodworm. Even the guard who stood at the door looked ill-equipped, in dingy clothes, holding a crooked spear.

"What did you expect, a grand ballroom?" Bird retorted.

I said nothing.

Little Jane, standing shakily behind us, looked pale. "What if she's not here?" she whispered.

"She'll be here," I said, with somewhat more conviction than I felt. And to Bird: "Where is the women's cell?"

He laughed. "There's just the one cell, Silvie."

I stared at him. "You mean they put a woman in there with—with the kinds of men they have to keep in prisons? Why, she's—" I pulled the dagger from its sheath at my side, all fear and hesitation gone. "We have to get her out of there, now."

Bird frowned. "And what kind of men are these, exactly?"

I turned on him, forgetting the knife I brandished until I saw him automatically step back from it; in that moment I didn't mind if I frightened him. "Thieves. Murderers. Brigands." I couldn't bring myself to say "rapists" with Little Jane right there, but Bird knew it as well as I.

He shook his head. "Men who've crossed your family, the sheriff, the king. That's the end and the size of it, Silvie. You'll see."

"Oh yes, because you see everything, don't you, Bird? Those men are all innocent, and my villainous brother is the devil incarnate? John is—he's—I don't approve of what he does, either, as well you know, and I don't even *like* him." I couldn't remember feeling defensive of John before, not ever, but the feeling ran hot in me now. "But just because he does bad things, Bird, that doesn't mean *everything* about him is bad! And my father committed some of these men to prison, too! You will not be telling me my father is the same kind of bully John has somehow become!"

"See, Silvie, it's not John you're defending now. It's your family. It's yourself. You want to believe you're not complicit in this, in all the ugly things nobles do." He took a step toward me. "It's not just your brother who's villainous, Silvie."

The knife felt hot in my hand. "Didn't I send out bread, Bird? Didn't I shoot the hart? Didn't I—" *Didn't I leave everything in my world, for the sake of Little Jane?*

And for my own sake, too.

I looked back at her, still pale and trembly, and I knew that I'd never done anything in my life that wasn't at least partly selfish.

I knew, too, that I shouldn't be worried about that right now.

"You said we needed to think of practicalities," I said. "Let's debate my family's and my class's merits later."

Bird opened his mouth, ready to say something, then looked at Little Jane and closed it again. He shrugged.

"Right," he said. "We have a midwife to jailbreak."

Bird stepped out from the shadows and greeted the guard with a friendly wave. "Simon," he said. "Good to see you."

"Bird!" The man stood and shook Bird's hand, and then mine as I stepped forward too. That was good: men always nodded to women, never shook their hands. Between the darkness, my hood and scarf, and the trousers I'd borrowed from Bird, I was well disguised.

"You've a lady guest, I think," Bird said. "The Mae."

Simon frowned. "Aye. Another one who couldn't pay on time, I thought at first; but then I realized she was clergy, and none of them pay tax at all. I didn't think they could be jailed, either—the Brethren Cardinals might as well be our second and third kings—but here Mae Tuck is, dragged in by none other than young Master John himself."

The word *complicit* rang in my head.

"She's to be kept for malicious falsehood, on his orders, and she's to stay here until his say-so." Simon shook his head. "You know as well as I do where arguing with the young master would get me. The lads inside like it no more than I—wouldn't be surprised if they tried to escape just for her sake. Mae Tuck brought half of them into this world, and the other half have wives or mothers or sisters who'd have died in childbed if not for her, or been saddled with babies they couldn't feed. She's as close to a saint as we get around here." Simon sighed. "But then, what am I telling you for? You know yourself the good she does."

Bird nodded, and I felt a twist in my gut as I wondered how exactly he'd encountered a midwife's services before.

"Well, you see, Simon, we've come to do your inmates' work for them," he said. "I've a girl here who is very much in need of Mae Tuck's help, and we won't be leaving before she gets it."

"I can't let her out," Simon said firmly. "Not when I'm the only one on duty. You know that. It's more than my head is worth, to be found disobeying the sheriff in such a fashion. But . . . your girl could come in to see the Mae, if she likes. I hate to think of any young one needing help as isn't getting it. You know I'd free her if I could, Bird . . . I'd free all of them, or nearly."

Bird nodded. "Hardly anyone'll be free after the king's harvest, the new taxes being what they are," he said. "Indeed, you might be the only one."

"Bring the girl in," Simon said. "I'll tell no one, I promise."

Little Jane stepped out of the shadows. She smiled tremulously.

"Little J—" Simon cut himself off, reddening. "Jane. Everyone's been wondering where you went."

Little Jane's hands clenched at her sides. "Has my father?"

Simon looked down. He shook his head and opened the jail's heavy door.

The smell inside stuck to my nose and tongue, so thick I could both taste and feel it. The source, a trough cut into the stone floor and running at a shallow incline toward an aperture in the far wall, was clear enough in the light of the lone torch on the wall; stale refuse still clung to it in places, and sticky rivulets of drying urine.

Beside me Little Jane tried to suppress a gag.

Almost every other inch of floor was covered by a sleeping or drowsing body. I couldn't believe how many people fit into this little cell. Five or six occupants would have crowded it, and I counted two dozen.

"John said it was rarely filled at all," I whispered. "He said it was foolish to keep paying the guard when the jail was empty."

Bird snorted.

Little Jane's efforts at suppressing her nausea came to nothing, and she let go of my hand to kneel over the trough and heave.

I bent down next to her to hold her hair away from her face, and when she was done, to rub her back and offer her my handkerchief. The smell of her sick barely registered among the other odors in the dank, sour room.

Simon came in with his lamp at last, and the sound of several bolts sliding closed followed him.

I felt a prickle on my skin as I heard the locks, and found my breath coming short. Such a small space, and to be trapped here, trapped . . . with men who had crossed my brother . . .

I wasn't trapped. I wasn't. No one here knew who I was, and as soon as Little Jane was seen to, the three of us would be free to go.

That so many others really were trapped here, I couldn't bear to think of.

"A girl here to see the Mae," Simon's voice called out, clear and firm, but not aggressive.

Nothing left in her to throw up, it seemed, Little Jane stood again, taking my handkerchief with a grateful nod and dabbing at her eyes before she wiped her mouth.

"Little Jane Carpenter?" A woman's voice came from the back of the room.

Simon held up his lamp, and Mae Tuck bustled her way carefully over the heaps of men.

I'd expected someone tall, perhaps not as tall as Jane or even myself, but . . . someone imposing. Yet the middle-aged woman who stepped forward was of a completely ordinary height, and in the lamplight her skin, eyes, and hair were all that grayish-dun you see on the fur of wild rabbits: a vanishing, camouflage color, made to pass beneath notice.

She wore the gray wimple that all Sistren wear, and her dress was firmly buttoned all the way up to her neck and down her sleeves, finishing over her thumbs so that it was almost as if she wore gloves.

But her partially covered hands were quick and steady, and when she reached out and took Jane's arm, I saw both kindness and authority in her touch. "Thank goodness you've found me," she said. "You had me worried when you ran away like that. You need someone looking after you —anyone in the condition does, and you're only a young one, my dear!"

Little Jane looked ashamed. "Mae Tuck, I didn't run away. I was . . ." She swallowed. "I didn't mean to run away," she finished quietly.

Mae Tuck pursed her lips. "Well, never mind. Let's have a look at you, and in a cleaner spot than this. I've a corner set up, for seeing to the lads' maladies." She glanced over her shoulder. "Boys? A little privacy for us ladies, if you wouldn't mind?"

In an instant these rough men, of whom I had been so

afraid, leapt to obey the Mae. They crowded closer together and faced discreetly away from the far corner of the little cell. One stone jutted out farther than the others from the wall there, and a small, squat pottery jug and some neatly folded scraps of fabric sat upon it.

"It's not my physic, but it gets me by," Mae Tuck said. "Simon, bless him, saw the sense in bringing me a few salves so I could keep the worst of the wounds in here from festering. It's only what I used to do before I was dragged in here myself, of course, and he was bright enough to say I could keep only what could easily be hidden in the event of a surprise inspection. Isn't that right, my boy?"

Simon nodded. "I won't tell you the state of this place, of the men inside, before Mae Tuck started looking after them," he said.

I was sure he was right: if the jail was that disgusting after the midwife's arrival, I couldn't even imagine what it'd been like before.

Mae Tuck led Little Jane into the corner. Bird and I turned away, too.

"I'm sorry to bother you like this, Mae, it's just I—I've been feeling a little weak, and I got afraid," I heard Little Jane say.

The Mae laughed. "Bother me, now? No such thing. All the bother I've had or am likely to have has come from our own dear young sheriff. You're no bother to me, Little Jane, nor ever could be. I doubt you've ever been a bother to anyone in all your life."

Little Jane didn't answer, but I heard the small catch in her breath. I knew she was thinking of her father.

"Now," Mae Tuck went on briskly, "let's have a look at you. Hmm, your pulse is fluttering true enough . . . When did you start feeling weak?"

I realized I was eavesdropping. Most of the men in the cell had taken up quiet conversations among themselves, those who hadn't already managed to fall back asleep; I decided to do the same with Bird.

"What did your mother have to say, in her note?" I whispered. "If you don't mind telling me, I mean." I couldn't quite bring myself to sit on the floor, so I leaned against the wall with him, the sides of our bodies touching.

"That she's proud of me. That she's glad I'm well, and that she is too, and not to worry about her." He took the paper out of his pocket and looked at it again. "That she's praying for all of us." He scanned the note, and it seemed as if there was more, but I didn't let myself even glance at her words. Soon enough Bird put the paper away, and he looked back up at me with an easy smile.

I smiled back at him.

Little Jane came toward us, smiling too, both hands resting on her belly. "Mae Tuck says I'm to eat more meat, as much as the baby and I can stand, and to find wild spin-ach and dandelion leaves when there's none to be had," she said. She made a face. "She said my blood went a bit thin, and it made me weak and dizzy, that's all. The baby and I share our blood, you know." She sounded knowledgeable, confident, and I was stunned at the difference that a few minutes of talking to the Mae had wrought in her.

I turned back toward the far corner, and I was about to curtsey to the midwife when I remembered myself and bowed instead, keeping a hand on the hem of my hood so it wouldn't slip. "Thank you, Mae," I said sincerely, pitching my voice low. "If I can ever do you any service—" But the courtly words died on my lips.

Perhaps I could indeed do her a service, a real one, if I only had the courage.

I just didn't know if I had.

The Mae nodded, touching two fingers to her heart and then gesturing toward my own, a typical blessing. I felt both grateful for it and ashamed.

"The service you can do me is to bring Little Jane back here in a week, and again a week after that," she said. "And to feed her well in the meantime; she needs to eat, even though she won't often feel hungry. Were we both still in the village I'd have her visit every day. I . . ." She sighed. "In fact, if you wouldn't mind a little crime, you could break into my annex at the parsonage and find a certain elixir, and give it to her to drink. It's only an extract of elderberry and ginger, but it will help with her nausea."

"Thank you, Mae," I said again, wishing I could thank her in a more meaningful way.

But I could. There was more courage in me than complicity, than submission to my brother. I'd started to find it when I sent bread to the people, when I shot the hart, when I took Little Jane—and myself—to freedom.

I should have known it in the clearing, or at the Hunt Ball, or indeed long before, but at least I knew it now. I was strong enough to oppose my brother.

I turned back to Simon, the guard and Bird's friend. I had to trust him—or rather, I knew that trusting him or not didn't matter.

"May I speak to you for a moment?" I asked. I could feel Bird looking at me quizzically, and I waved him away. "Go on outside," I told my two companions. "I'm sure you're longing for the fresh air, and I'll catch up with you there."

"But, Sil—" Bird stopped himself just in time, and before he was able to call me by any other name Little Jane was already headed for the door, practically sprinting. I knew he'd feel duty-bound to follow her out.

I looked around the dank cell. "I want to take the Mae with us," I said to Simon. "For Little Jane's good. Please."

Simon smiled sadly. "And I want to send her with you,

honest," he said. "I'd nearly do it, too, if it were only myself at stake. But you clearly don't know the young sheriff here, if you'll excuse my saying it. He's the type to punish you sideways, through the ones you love. I hope you understand."

"But say you had permission—or a command, I mean—from someone else in the Abbey, from another Loughsley? Surely you could let the Mae go then, and John could do nothing about it."

Simon eyed me sharply. "If you're thinking of petitioning the family, you won't get far," he said slowly. "The old master is . . . ill, has been so for a long time. His mind is weak, and even when it wasn't . . . he never met with petitioners from the village, only fellow nobles. And the only other Loughsley is—was—his daughter, but there's been some kind of scandal with her, too, something the young sheriff's made sure to keep hushed up. My mother works in the Abbey, and she tells me the girl is gone."

"She's not gone far," I said. I lowered my hood. My brown skin and dark blond hair would mark me as a Loughsley right away, even if Simon had never seen my face.

I was half expecting a gasp, but he didn't look surprised. "I'd say not," he said, leaning back and crossing his arms over his chest. He looked me up and down, and then he began to laugh. "You're no Little Jane, but you're tall enough

I didn't think twice about your being a lad," he said. "The more fool I! At least, not until you said your brother's name that way."

"What way?"

"So familiar, so knowing, but . . ." He stopped himself. "No common man would say a lord's first name so casually. And you're not from our own village, so how would you even know the sheriff's name?"

I nodded. "That was a slip; I'll be more careful next time. Thank you for telling me." I glanced back at the door. "Then you'll let me take the Mae?"

He sighed heavily. "Mistress, it would please me greatly," he said. "And I don't think John could argue with it himself, stickler for the letter of the law as he is . . . if only I could prove it was you gave me the order."

"Ah." I tried to think. "Of course."

"No chance you'd come back in the morning to tell him yourself, I imagine?"

He asked the question drily, but I still felt embarrassed. I couldn't say what it was exactly that I feared so much about seeing John again, but something had fundamentally changed in our relationship now that I had escaped him once, and I felt certain deep in my bones that I didn't want to know what would happen if we met again.

"Piece of paper?" I asked.

He shook his head. "Couldn't use it if I had it, my lady — not to write on, anyway."

I blinked, trying not to show my surprise.

"There's not many outside castles or churches who can read and write, you know," he told me, not unkindly.

"Well, if there's anything I could write on at all . . . John would know my signature, you see. My way of writing," I explained.

Simon looked around. "I've some whitewash here," he said. "Was going to repaint the cell in the morning. Gets dingy real quickly."

"I believe it," I said, smiling. I was starting to have a rather theatrical idea.

❧❦

Bird leaned forward with his hands on his thighs. He'd barely stopped laughing since we'd left the jail the night before, and he'd woken up laughing still.

"It's like an old ballad!" he said between attacks. "Couldn't you have used a sword, for real effect?"

"You know I'm hopeless at swordplay," I said. "John'd never recognize my writing if I did it that way." I grinned.

"Say it again," Bird said, wiping his eyes.

I sighed, but it was such fun to make Bird laugh, and in this case, so easy.

"'As daughter of Loughsley, I have freed the Mae of this village, Sara Tuck. I will do all in my power to free any who are subject to injustice here.' And then I signed my name."

Bird burst into laughter again.

"I don't see what exactly is funny," I said. "Did I say something foolish?"

Bird managed to get his breath back, but he was still grinning widely. "Not foolish at all," he said. "It's beautiful. It's just I keep picturing John's face when he reads it—" He stopped himself from laughing again. "What you wrote, it's perfect. 'Any who are subject to injustice' . . . Silvie, that's everyone in the kingdom. You've promised to free us all. And it won't just be John who gets that message: everyone in the village will. It makes me—love you, even more than I do, anyway, and feel so proud of you. So proud."

Our eyes met, and that warmth began to steal up between us again, the heat that suggested a kind of love that wasn't just that born of more than a decade's friendship. A kind of love I wasn't ready for, because it meant risking that friendship, and risking the freedom that I'd given up so much to achieve.

I looked away from Bird, and down at the fire.

"Let's have tea," I said, "now that we've a kettle, and real tea leaves, at least for the time being."

Bird shot me an odd look. "We have them forever, or for

as long as you want them," he said. "They're yours for the taking, remember?"

I shrugged. "I suppose." I still wanted to believe we would be able to survive out here, on our own, free from Loughsley. Free from everything.

As always, Bird seemed to read my mind. "I'll take my lass for a hunt," he said. "We need to do our part to keep meat on the table, too."

"What table?" I said, smiling. "And what do you mean? If it weren't for your cooking, Little Jane and I would have eaten our boar raw, or burned to ashes, as well you know." *And if it weren't for you, we would neither of us be living free and hunting boar in the forest at all,* I thought.

We shared another look. I knew I didn't have to say that, either.

Bird shook his head. "You'd have figured it out," he said, pouring water into the kettle. "Now go and see how Little Jane is getting on with the Mae, if you like, and I'll bring the tea out to you."

He was turned away from me, toward the coals of the fire. As he stoked them the red light flared across his hair, turning it briefly the color of rubies. I wanted to reach out, to run my fingers through that deep red . . .

I left Bird and walked into the dappled green brightness outside.

Mae Tuck and Little Jane were by the stream, my tall

friend sitting with her bare feet in the current. The Mae crouched next to her, skirts girded, lifting water from the stream in her cupped hands and pouring it slowly over Little Jane's calves. Little Jane's eyes were closed, and her face was relaxed.

"Ladies," I said in greeting, "how are you getting on?"

Little Jane opened her eyes, blinking a few times. "I don't know how I managed without the Mae, even before I was with child," she said, sighing and leaning back farther on her elbows. "I've never felt so cared for in my life."

Mae Tuck shook her head, beginning to gently massage the muscles in Little Jane's legs. "Everyone needs caring for," she said.

Jane's saying she had never been looked after struck my heart, but something else she'd said moved me more.

She had never actually said she was with child before. She'd never once used the words. And what I saw on her face wasn't just relaxation, I realized: it was acceptance.

"I want you to know," I told Mae Tuck, "first of all that you are welcome here, with us, for as long as you want to stay. But if there's any way that we can help you get back to your home, anything that I can do as the daughter of Loughsley to restore your good standing—I'll do it. We'll help you however we can, I promise."

Mae Tuck kept her eyes on her patient. "Is that better?" she asked.

My friend sighed in satisfaction. "Oh yes. All the swelling's gone, I think." She pulled her feet out of the stream and wiped them on the hem of her dress.

"We'll do that every morning, so, and there will be compresses for you when the stream freezes over," the Mae said. "And we'll get some fish for you to eat. Salmon, if we can."

She then turned to me. "Thank you, my child," she said. "Thank you for what you did last night, for my own sake and for the sake of this young mother here. The village of Woodshire is small, as you know, and it has only gotten smaller in my time. Little Jane is the patient I have most worried about, ever since she came to me four months ago. The other women who are with child now all have had children before, and — well, families who are minding them. I am very grateful to you for bringing us together again."

She arched her shoulders and raised her arms above her head, stretching. "I've been waiting for a sign from above, from the Lady, to tell me it's time to move on from Woodshire's parsonage. I didn't think it would come so soon, especially once I was jailed; I thought she was telling me to do my work there, and certainly there was plenty of healing to be done. But I know now that she was bringing me to you." She took my hand. Her own was still wet and cool from the stream. "Yes, I will stay here with you, at least until Little Jane has birthed her baby. Then we will see what the Lady says. The Mae are a mendicant order, you know."

I smiled at her reference to the Lady; it was antiquated now, almost quaint. The Brethren taught that the Lord was God, and I'd only learned about his Lady — always "his" — in some of the stories I'd heard at church, or from my nurses or tutors. But even in those stories she'd never been powerful enough to send visions or signs.

"I thought that most Sistren were cloistered," I said, remembering something else from those stories. "Aren't Mae a kind of Sistren?" I'd had a Sistren governess once, a cold and strict woman who had always made it clear that she longed to return to her nunnery, and not have to teach theology to loud and sticky children.

Mae Tuck, sitting by the stream and smiling as she massaged Little Jane's swollen feet and spoke of the Lady's signs, could not have been more different from that severe Sister.

"The Mae are one of many Sistren orders. Most Sistren *are* cloistered, these days," Mae Tuck acknowledged, "and many more than used to be — but that's a story for another day. The Mae are simply traveling midwives, really. We go where the Lady tells us we are needed." She looked up at the canopy, her dun-colored eyes still twinkling, and then she looked behind me. Her smile grew. "Yes, I think that for now to stay with you is exactly what I should do, my child."

I looked behind me to see what she was smiling about. Bird was approaching us, a steaming mug in each hand. "Sugar in it and everything, though we've no milk," he said.

"For you, Mae Tuck." He gave her one mug with a respectful nod.

He brought the other mug to Little Jane, and handed it to her with a gentleness that filled my heart with affection for them both. I trotted back to the cave to pour tea for me and for Bird into two horn cups I'd brought along with the Loughsley supplies the night before. I took no sugar myself, but I added four cubes to Bird's tea.

At his first sip he raised his eyebrows.

"I remember you always liked it sweet, when we were little," I said. "Your mother used to tease you."

"She said I needed something to keep me sweet," he recalled. "When I got old enough to realize she couldn't always buy me sugar, I trained myself out of liking it. I've drunk it black for years." He looked up, his cheeks flushing. "But this is good, Silvie. I'd just made myself forget how much I like sweet tea, that's all."

"I would have given you sugar, Bird," I said.

He shook his head and took another long sip. "We'll spare it for the winter now," he said. "We need all the food to last as long as possible. I'm glad I've trained myself out of it, really. But that makes this even more of a treat."

"A treat indeed," said Mae Tuck. "I must teach you how to make bramble wine out here, in exchange. I'll toast us with this, if you don't mind, Silviana."

Her deference to me was unsettling, even more so

than Little Jane's had been. I was no leader. "Of course," I said.

She raised her mug, and the three of us followed suit, Little Jane coming to stand on the Mae's right-hand side so that we formed a kind of circle.

"To three brave young people who know their own hearts," she said. "May you always have the courage of your convictions."

As we drank I heard a familiar flutter. Bird's falcon landed in front of the cave, a fair-sized salmon clutched in her beak. And even though Mae Tuck hadn't said a prayer, or mentioned the Lord or the Lady at all in her toast, it still had the ring about it of a blessing.

# ~EIGHT~

## Scarlet and Much

That night, Bird slept alone by the mouth of the cave. He said nothing about it, but as he walked past me while we all were bedding down he briefly touched my shoulder. When I looked up I saw something in his eyes that might have been apology, or sadness, or longing. I wanted it to be the latter, and I didn't; but without Bird next to me, even at the end of that long night, I found I couldn't sleep.

Mae Tuck seemed to have settled down in her new surroundings with total ease: she snored soundly. Little Jane and Bird slept like stones.

After endless hours of lying in wait for sleep that wouldn't come, I rose and walked to the hot spring at the back of the cave. I slipped off the trousers and men's shirt I still wore: laundry in the forest was an ordeal involving frigid river water, the labor of wringing out heavy, sopping fabric, and drying for days on end over the fire. We wore the same clothes until they were truly dirty, something that seemed normal to Bird and Little Jane but had offended all the aristocratic sensibility I had left. I'd never worn the same dress two days in a row in all my life, at Loughsley Abbey; I'd only even dressed myself there because I preferred my privacy to the assistance of a lady's maid.

Well, I had privacy now, in this place I shared with three deeply sleeping friends, and I felt no shyness at all as I removed the rest of my clothing and stepped in. The warm water felt heavy and rich on my bare skin, much like the fine gowns I'd left behind. In the dim red light of Bird's banked fire, the ripples on the surface gleamed like jewels.

I sank back into the spring. Every sore muscle in my body sighed.

My eyes fluttered closed, but my mind felt clearer and more awake than it had all day. The water was just deep enough that I could let my legs float, that I felt carried. Cradled.

Complete darkness and warmth, privacy and safety. Alone unto myself, but with the comforting presence of those I loved nearby.

I wondered, resting there, if Little Jane's baby was dreaming, too.

❧ ❧

I stayed in the hot spring through the beginning of dawn. Bird was the first to stir, and I was too lulled by the heat and the water to leap for my clothes as he stood up. It was still half-dark inside the cave, anyway, I told myself — but I knew, some part of me knew, that I wouldn't mind if it had been bright.

He turned toward where I should have been sleeping, and I watched surprise and apprehension move through the lines of his body when he didn't find me there. "Silvie . . ."

"I'm here, Bird." My voice sounded low, husky, even to my own ears, as if it had gone bathing, too.

"Silvie—" His body told me the moment he knew where I was. He turned discreetly away. "Did you sleep well?" he asked, his voice barely above a whisper. "I'll come back to you tonight, if you want me to. But I thought — I can make hammocks for us with the cloth from the sacks we brought back. I only thought, with the Mae here now . . ."

"No, you were right." I knew well that I should learn to sleep without him again. We'd be up in the trees soon, any-way . . . and while I cared less than I likely ought to about what Mae Tuck or anyone else might think of our sleeping arrangements, I had come to the woods chasing freedom. If I turned out to need Bird out here even more than I had at Loughsley, how free was I? How bound?

I reached for my cloak. "Hammocks would be perfect, at least until we're in the trees," I said. I dried off and dressed again, and I resigned myself to sleeping alone.

When Bird came back to the cave the next evening,

he brought something with him. Not a rabbit or another salmon, but we hardly minded. The strips of boar drying over the fire still seemed like more than we'd eat in a month, and the previous day's fish combined with some dandelion greens Mae Tuck and I had foraged had been a veritable feast—and the cheese and grain at the back of the cave were like gold in a treasury.

I felt guilty remembering my hesitation the first time I left Loughsley. If I'd gotten over my pride, my murky fear, and gone back earlier to take the food I would have freely eaten in my own house, we would never have gone hungry. And maybe Little Jane would not have gotten sick.

"Gifts for you, Silvie, Little Jane," Bird said, with an apologetic nod toward Mae Tuck. "There were only two of them, Mae, and I didn't know if you'd like to . . . to hunt." Then, looking back at us, "Their mother's died. They need looking after, and my lass could always use helpers." Seraph ruffled her feathers.

He pulled two gray dust balls from the leather satchel at his side. That was what they looked like, anyway: scraggly things, little more than ill-organized piles of speckled down.

But when he held them up and the firelight touched them, a pair of angry yellow eyes glared out of each ball. Tiny beaks opened and closed with protesting clacks. The owlets cheeped imperiously, protesting the light.

"Oh, Bird," Little Jane murmured, reaching out and

taking one from him, cupping it against her cheek. "Oh, he's lovely."

Bird handed the other owlet to me. It was so soft and light I could barely feel it in my hands, except for its thrumming heartbeat.

"This one's a female," he told me as he handed her off. "They're the better hunters, but don't tell that small lad, or he'll feel inferior."

"Inferior nothing!" Little Jane said, stroking her owlet's downy head. He glowered around at the room in general before he submitted to the petting. After a few moments his eyes half closed in sleepy contentment.

Mine pecked at the drawstring of my cloak. No amount of petting was softening her glare, but I rather liked her for it. And her fierce yellow eyes, reflecting the fire, held some of the deep ruby redness that Bird's hair had the day before.

"I'll call her Scarlet," I said, scratching under her beak. Scarlet seemed to like that a little better, although she still looked at me as if I had dishonored her family. I took a little scrap of meat from the bone I'd been gnawing and held it up to her.

She snatched it so fast I hardly caught the movement. Although she still glared, there was something in her imperious manner that suggested I might be permitted to keep giving her food, if I didn't get too cocky about it.

"Well, mine's a lovey," said Little Jane. Her owlet had

already fallen asleep in her hand, his head lolling a bit to the side, reduced to just a dust ball again with his huge eyes closed.

"They don't look like much when you can't see their eyes," I said.

"Then I'll call mine Much," said Little Jane, "for he's so small, and there's so much of me—especially lately." She laughed. As we all laughed with her, it was Mae Tuck's eye I caught. Could she see all the good she had already done for my friend?

Little Jane brushed her cheek softly across the sleeping Much's head. "We balance each other out that way," she said.

❧❧

It was a struggle not to spend the whole of the next day cooing over my new little charge, but the specter of winter haunted us every moment. Several times as I gathered plants and herbs with Mae Tuck and hung them for drying I stopped, trying not to shiver, certain that I could taste snow in the air.

I'd never felt so close to the seasons before. I remembered Clara saying at the Hunt Ball that the seasons hardly came to the city at all, that she didn't know how I could bear them out here in the wilderness . . . I'd known then that she only meant to convince herself of how superior the court was, but I hadn't realized how wrong she was.

Every month of every year of my life in Loughsley Abbey I was wrapped in warmth and comfort. The seasons affected only which fruits and meats were served at our table, and whether the visiting nobles would hunt or fish, or skate on the frozen river. Which colors I saw out my window.

Out here winter wasn't a meal, a charming pastime, a color.

It was a threat.

❧ ⚜ ❧

Every night, in the cave, that threat receded. Bird's fire would mellow to coals over the course of the day while we were building, but it never quenched. In fact, the fire hadn't gone out since he'd kindled it on our first night in the forest . . . nearly a month before. It didn't seem possible we'd been here so long when I looked at the rising moon through the trees; it was just a sliver past new, exactly as it had been when we arrived. My flux had come on me again, too. It had just ended when I ran away, and I hadn't thought, and then I'd been grateful for the Mae's advice on how to manage it out here. There was no denying the time gone by.

"We should mark the occasion somehow," I told Bird and Little Jane, carefully prodding the tubers I was roasting at the edge of the coals. Bird had built up the center of the fire again, and there, in the old cauldron he'd brought here years ago, simmered a rabbit his falcon had caught, fragrant with the herbs Mae Tuck and I had picked together.

I had never felt the cold so much in my old life, but sitting around the fire with these three, I thought I'd never felt warmth so much, either.

Scarlet hooted indignantly in my pocket. I stroked her head, soft as a cloud, and fed her a tiny shred of the rabbit's offal. That morning, Little Jane had fed Much a mouse that had unwisely invaded our grain stores during the night. The way the scrawny owlet gulped down the whole mouse was . . . impressive, but I found myself squeamish at the idea of feeding my charge live meat.

Scarlet swallowed the rabbit's stomach and chirruped. She blinked her huge, outraged eyes, then fluffed her feathers, eyeing the darkness beyond the fire at the cave's mouth.

I smiled at her, wondering how I could grow so fond of any creature this quickly. I was like Clara fretting over Titan! I'd never wanted a pet at Loughsley. I loved riding, but that was for its freedom; I never longed for a pony or a puppy of my own, the way some children did. I'd seen too many dogs and cats mistreated, whether by bullies like John who hurt them, or by simpering courtiers like Clara, who kept them so drugged that they were no more than toys. I'd hated the idea of being so responsible for a fellow creature's happiness or misery.

Beside me, Little Jane tucked Much into the nest of sacking and moss we had made for the owlets. Scarlet's pin feathers were coming in, but she still wasn't big enough to fly out at night. I settled her down next to her brother, to rest if not to sleep, and to keep their owly watch over us.

Little Jane retrieved a small, heavy-looking bag from a shadowy corner of the cave. She poured its contents onto her lap and began sorting through them: nails, long and short, all of them fat and sturdy. "We'll need them come building-time, and that's sooner than I thought, with the dry weather we've been having," she said quietly when she caught me watching her. "I thought, you know, that I've as much right to the nails in the carpenter's shed as you have to Loughsley's kitchen stores, Silvie."

"At least as much," I said. "The nails are sorely needed, I know, but . . . take someone with you, the next time you want to raid the carpentry. We're safer together—"

"Good evening," came a deep voice behind us.

My heart jumped so high in my throat that for a moment I thought I'd be sick.

I leapt off the ground and spun to face the cave's entrance, cursing myself for leaving my bow and arrows by my bed.

The others stood, too, Little Jane making two fists and towering above the rest of us, Bird suddenly holding a curved hunting knife. I remembered the dagger in my sheath then, too late to take it out stealthily. I saw Bird look at my empty hands and shoot me one quick, frustrated look, over so quickly it almost hadn't happened.

Only Mae Tuck rose slowly. When she faced the cave entrance with us, her face was as open and kind as ever.

"Who's there?" I called into the darkness beyond the fire.

"The Lord and Lady bless all here!" a deep voice replied. Three people appeared out of the gloom: an older man and woman and a girl of about sixteen, all dressed in rough peasant clothes. The man had a bushy brown beard threaded heavily with gray. The woman wore a scarf over her head. The girl's shiny nut-brown hair spilled out of her own scarf, and she had a pretty, rosy, round-cheeked face. Her eyes were wide with fright at first, but she looked past me at Bird, and a smile of recognition overtook her.

"Forgive us for startling you," said the man. "We mean no harm. The truth is, Mistress Loughsley, we need your help." He made me an unpracticed bow, and the two next to him quickly followed with equally awkward curtsies.

Bird stepped forward, lowering his knife. The girl's rosy

cheeks grew yet rosier, and I thought the strength of the smile she was giving him might break her face.

I was still watching her when Bird spoke, so I missed his first few words.

". . . you to come so far, Kent?" I glanced at him; his face was still wary. "And how did you find us?"

"It was my daughter who guessed where you'd be," the man said.

The girl giggled. "Don't you remember when you took me here, Bird?" she asked. "When I heard from Katie up in the Abbey about you and the lady vanishing, I figured this is where you'd hide."

I started to feel sick. I scolded myself: how dare I think Bird should only have come here with me, when we were children? We had never promised each other exclusivity, even in friendship. How dare I begrudge him other friends? I had forgotten the cave, our castle, entirely. And this rosy, pretty girl who was fairly glowing at Bird: she remembered.

I couldn't look at her, so I kept my eyes on her father instead. He set down a lumpy, heavy-looking sack. "I knew well what'd befall us, if we stayed in the village," he said. "The jailhouse for me. The young sheriff's raised Woodshire's taxes again, and if rumors are true, the king will soon do the same. I've little enough work as it is, for . . ."

"For who can hire a stonemason, when there's no one with money for building," Bird finished quietly.

"Aye. That's about the size of it. And I won't leave my family hungry while I rot in that damnable place. But we saw—" The man chuckled, and he made me another rough bow. "We saw what you did to the jailhouse's wall, mistress, and it's a mighty thing if ever I saw one. I couldn't read it, of course, but Nellie here did and told us, and oh, if we didn't laugh ourselves into stitches! If there's someone standing up to the young sheriff, telling him nay for once in his bully's life, then that's someone I want to stand with. So we need your help, but we'll stand with you, too. We believe in what it is you're doing, mistress." And he made me his deepest bow yet.

*I'm not doing anything,* I wanted to say—I wanted to scream it. *I'm not standing up to John. I'm not that brave. I ran away!*

But I knew these people didn't care about that. What they needed was a kind of help we could give them. That was all that mattered. Not my cowardice, not the jealousy I felt nipping at me as the daughter radiated her smiles toward Bird. All that mattered was how I might help them.

I stepped forward and took the hand of the stonemason's wife in my own. "Of course you can stay with us, for as long as you need," I said. She still didn't speak, but she nodded slowly and closed her eyes. When she opened them again I could see that she was almost crying.

I felt suddenly embarrassed. I looked over at Little Jane, and she smiled at the man Bird had called Kent.

"I was just saying we need more hands as know building," she said.

# ~NINE~

## *Tree Houses*

When I woke up the next morning, pleased with myself to find that the light outside the cave still held a little of the pink of dawn, the stonemason's daughter, Nellie, was tending the fire. Everyone else was gone.

"Where's Bird?" I asked, stretching my arms above my head as I sat up. We'd slept apart since Mae Tuck had joined our group, but somehow I still expected to find him next to me each morning.

"He's gone to help cut timber," the girl said, settling our kettle onto its long hook and chain, then carefully letting go so that it didn't swing or splash before coming to rest above the hottest part of the fire. It was a practiced, easy motion. She'd tended fires and boiled water all her life, I supposed, so why shouldn't she be good at it? But something about her ease bothered me.

"I promised him I'd keep the fire going. He seemed fair concerned about it, too." She laughed softly to herself.

I made myself relax my shoulders and loosen my face into a friendly smile before I spoke to her again. She had come here with her parents because they needed friends, after all. Why should I feel anything but friendship toward her? Why should I care that she'd promised anything to Bird?

I blinked. I didn't care, of course.

"That was good of you," I said, standing up. "Bird thinks we'll all freeze to death the minute the fire quenches, you see."

I laughed, but she didn't laugh with me. Instead, she prodded the coals again. "He's not wrong, mistress," she said, "especially here, inside damp stone like you are. Even a stone cottage gets horrible cold in the winter, if the fire's out for just one day, or one night. Mam always tells me my most important job, when she's not at home, is keeping the hearth lit. The house can be a mess, and no food on the table, long as the fire's going strong."

The girl's chin trembled at the thought of home. I stepped toward her, suddenly finding her much more sympathetic than I had a moment before.

"Well, you're just the right one for the job, then, Nellie," I said. We smiled at each other.

"Has Little Jane been with you all along?" she asked. "I worried about her when she left the village, and her parents wouldn't say where she'd gone. Her father kept saying a girl as big as her could make her own way in the world, and not to worry, but . . . I did."

"She's been with us," I said. "It's a great blessing to have her, too. She killed a boar that's still feeding us, and it's because of her we'll have tree houses to sleep in come winter, instead of the cave. And she's lovely company. A lovely friend."

"She is. I was almost as glad to see her again as . . . well." Nellie brushed back the loose hair that had fallen from her kerchief. "I thought you and Bird had run off *together*, you see." She looked at me hopefully.

I despised myself a little for it, but I couldn't quite bring myself to tell her it wasn't that way between Bird and me. "Ah . . . what's your mother's name, by the way? I don't think she told us last night," I said. It was the first question I could think of that had nothing to do with romance.

"Nell. I'm named for her. She'd have told you her name herself, only she can't speak."

I hid my surprise—or so I thought, but Nellie laughed at my expression. "It's not that uncommon, after the whoop that came through ten years ago. Not uncommon in the villages, leastways, mistress."

That made me remember myself, and why I had asked her name in the first place. "Please, call me Silvie," I said. "No one out here calls me anything else—I don't want them to. I'm nobody's mistress out here." That was starting to feel like a mantra. "I'm sorry about your mother's voice. Is there any way I can—that is—" I wasn't sure how to go on.

Nellie laughed again, and the brilliant smile that I'd thought was just for Bird broke out on her face once more. "Ask her yourself," she said.

❧ ❧

"One, two, pull!" Little Jane called.

With a deep creaking and groaning sound, the stack of wood on the ground rose into the air. I couldn't see the vines that supported it at first, although I knew they must be there; for a moment it seemed as if the force of Little Jane's voice alone compelled it to move. "One, two, pull!" she called again.

This time I caught the sliding movement of vines through the shadows of the branches. In the dappled forest light, glinting around masses of crisp, colored leaves and ivy and moss and sweeping, low-hanging branches, it was almost impossible to see them.

"One, two, pull!"

I could hear labored breathing behind the creak of the vines and the load they bore, behind the rustle of the trees and falling leaves, behind the sound of the wind that swept its way above behind the rush of the river. Kent the stonemason, his wife, Nell, and even Mae Tuck were lined up and putting all their weight into lifting the heavy load.

But where was Bird?

"One, two, pull!"

"That's grand, so!" called a familiar voice from somewhere up there in the ocean of autumn fire.

I couldn't see Bird, but hearing him was a comfort.

"We should be able to get them unloaded and set down the floor frame here."

I went to the nearest trunk, a sturdy hundred-year-old oak, grabbed a branch just above my head, and swung myself up.

In a few movements I was as high as Bird, I was sure of it. But I couldn't see him; when I looked down, I couldn't see the ground for all the overlapping branches and leaves and vines and mosses beneath me.

"You're there?" I called in no particular direction.

"Silvie?"

Ah. I straightened myself up to standing and walked forward across one sturdy branch, then found another when the first one grew thin and started to bend under my weight. Like the climbing, this was a knack I hadn't lost since I was a child, and it filled me with a simple happiness: balancing, walking from branch to branch, pushing greenery away from my face like parting curtains as I went.

And behind the last curtain was Bird.

He had taken the top piece from the stack of timber and walked it out from the trunk of his tree, an oak so thick it could have fit every one of our party inside its base, even with our three newcomers. Now he was positioning it between two extended branches, where it would form part of the frame of our new home.

"Hi, Silvie," he said, looking up at me with a half grin. "Hold that end steady while I tack this one, will you?"

I hopped onto Bird's tree, holding the wood with both hands. I felt the vibration of Bird's hammer strikes coming through the timber, and a splinter or two began to wedge their way into my palms. But I didn't mind: we were making a new house, a new home; we really were. Soon we wouldn't be trapped in the cave anymore; soon we'd live every moment in the freedom of the treetops, even while we slept. I thrilled to the idea.

Besides, the splinters might help me. I was ready to have, like Little Jane and Mae Tuck and even Nellie and her silent mother, the toughened hands of a woman who works.

❧ ❧

My palms blistered instead of growing hard and callused. By the time dusk had grown too deep for us to keep working, they were pink, swollen, and weeping, and I couldn't even close my hands enough to make a fist.

I tried to keep them hidden, but Bird saw them. His

eyes widened at the bloody marks I left on the last of the timber we handled that day. I thought I might be in for another lecture.

"Oh, Silvie," he murmured, stepping close to me in the gray shadows and taking my right hand delicately in his, the same way I'd seen him handling Scarlet and Much the day before.

"It's nothing—" I started, but he let go and I heard a ripping sound, and then Bird was winding a strip of cotton around my palm, wrapping it in layers from my thumb to the first knuckle of my four fingers.

"Just to help protect them when you're climbing down," he said. "Then you should ask Mae Tuck to dress them properly for you." He took up my other hand and wrapped that one, too. Just the relief of the fabric, of a shield between the pulsing ache in my hands and the raw air, was so wonderful that I couldn't even think to protest about his tending to me too much.

Cupping my mummified hands in his two callused palms, he raised one to his face and kissed the bandage.

"Now, that should help a little. Just until Mae Tuck can see to it, mind." He spoke as casually as if he hadn't just kissed me at all.

Then he climbed down the trunk, leaving me blinking. I could feel my quickened heartbeat in the throbbing of my hands.

Getting down was still painful enough that I had to bite the inside of my cheek to keep from crying out. Without Bird's bandages it would have been intolerable. They were soaked through with fluid by the time I reached the bottom of the tree, but Mae Tuck was already waiting there for me. She carefully unwound the cloth and tutted over the torn and swollen skin, then led me to the numbing coldness of the stream.

After all, I thought, as the icy water blessedly stole all the feeling from my hands, Bird hadn't broken our agreement; he hadn't kissed me, only a bandage—the fabric of his own shirt. That was nothing, just as it was nothing when we slept curled together in the cave each night . . . or when we had done, before the Mae and the Masons arrived.

I missed sleeping with Bird. I could admit that much, if only to myself. I couldn't quite admit that I wished he'd break our promise.

## ~TEN~

# Band of Rogues

We roasted two rabbits for the supper that night, and Bird basted them with wine as he turned them on the fire. The smell was as lovely and suggestive as a good dream. I still couldn't believe how hungry I was at the end of each day.

The joy of good food and of the company around the fire was nearly enough to make me forget my aching hands, too, especially now that Mae Tuck had painted a mint salve onto my blisters.

"Take the bandages off in the morning, if you can bear it," she told me. "Once you're up in the trees, of course. If you can push through these few days you'll be well on your way to having skin like leather gloves." She wiggled the fingers of her own well-hardened hands and smiled at me.

I smiled back. "What would my governesses say?"

"Or the Sistren in the convents?" She laughed. "They're supposed to swear off vanity, but oh, you should see how they mind their smooth hands. Of course, it's the Brethren who make them that way, but even so . . . no lady's soft fingers for me, thank you."

I took a big bite of the spit-roasted rabbit. "What do you mean, 'the Brethren make them that way'?" I asked, wiping the juices from my lips with my sleeve. None of my governesses would know me now, that was certain.

Mae Tuck sighed. "You wouldn't believe the things they tell the novices, the young girls going in to be cloistered. Through their hands they do the Lord's work, and so they must keep them pure and soft and untouched by anything rough or earthly. The Sistren are the Lord's wives, you see; when you take your vows, you marry God. So it's their whole bodies they're meant to keep soft and untouched — but the Brethren find it more polite to speak of their hands, and just to keep them locked up. Out of sight, out of mind." She shook her head. "They've been trying to cloister the Mae for centuries, and it's nearly worked. I shouldn't wonder, the kind of work we do. They speak of the holy blood of the Lord, but they'd faint at the sight of human blood. They speak of keeping the body pure and holy, but I think if one of them ever really saw the workings of a woman's body, the purity and holiness that's truly there, they'd die of fright."

I had to laugh. "Mae Tuck, you're giving a sermon!"

She chuckled and took a deep draught from her cup of bramble wine; she'd just opened the first of our batches that morning. "Lady and Lord, I am. No more of that."

She swallowed, then reached for one of the tubers at the edge of the coals. Her callused hands picked it up without flinching, and I determined to keep my bandages off all the following day, no matter the pain.

"To practical conversation," she said, raising her cup.

I touched my own mug to it, smiling. "To holy blood," I answered, "and to women, too."

I must have spoken louder than I thought, because Bird looked up at us from across the fire. "I'll drink to that," he said, and he did, with a wink to us both.

∾⟊ ⟊∾

Nellie slept at the rear of the cave with Little Jane, their two hammocks strung in a row like hanging fruit; the bags in which the Masons had brought their few belongings had soon been repurposed for sleeping. Mae Tuck still slept in just her cloak and shawl, on a bed of moss near their feet; she said she'd grown used to hard beds as a novice, and wouldn't be able to sleep on a mattress or hammock if she tried. Bird slept on the ground by the fire, but on the opposite side from me, guarding the entrance; he insisted he preferred sleeping on stone, although I crossly suspected him of being chivalrous. Kent and Nell Mason had refused hammocks, too, choosing instead to bed down together on the moss where Bird and I had once slept.

"We've never slept apart since we were married," Kent said, "and we're too old to be starting now. Besides, this one sleepwalks. Liable to trample all of you if we're not holding hands through the night."

Nell colored and gave her husband a smart smack across the shoulder, then opened her mouth in a silent laugh and leaned over to kiss the place she'd hit. Kent put his arm around her and returned the kiss, softly, on her forehead.

I glanced at Bird without meaning to and saw him watching them with a smile and a sadness in his eyes at the same time. But then he caught me looking, and he turned to tend the fire.

The hammock was a vast improvement over the hard, damp cave ground; my back was dry, and the curve of the fabric was like being cradled in a gigantic, benevolent hand. But I still found it hard to drift off. I'd never been able to sleep on my back, always feeling too exposed to some nameless nightmare, but the hammock wouldn't let me curl up in my usual sideways ball; I had to keep my legs stretched out, or the fabric would twist in on itself and I'd take a tumble. So I lay first on my right side, then on my left, trying unsuccessfully to find comfort, and fighting with the hammock to keep my balance every time I moved.

Finally I faded into unquiet dreams. The cave grew richly appointed, even more so than my chamber at Loughsley had been: it was like a room inside a palace. I lay in bed wearing a silver gown that glowed like moonlight. The bodice and the sleeves were too tight.

As I moved to get up, they only grew tighter, and my voluminous skirts tangled around my legs, tying me down. Then I saw that the sheets and canopy were glowing like moonlight too, and their fabric was the same as my gown, and I wasn't wearing a gown at all but was naked in bed, unable to move, and someone was coming toward the door—a faceless bridegroom, a monster whose face I would die upon seeing—and I tried to scream, but the silver sheets filled my mouth and I could make no sound, the silk was pushing into my lungs and I couldn't breathe, couldn't breathe—

"Silvie, wake up. Silvie."

I opened my eyes with a strangled gasp. There was a dark shape above me, a person, but I knew it wasn't a monster, not anyone who would do me harm.

"Bird." I reached out, and the relief of knowing that no shining silk tied my arms down was so great that I felt tears start in my eyes. I touched Bird's cheek. There was just enough light from the fire that I could watch him close his eyes and lean against my hand. "Bird, I was dreaming . . ."

"I know. I'm sorry to wake you." He didn't understand. I shook my head, wanting to explain, but he went on before I could.

"There are people outside. I've woken Kent and Nell. The others . . ."

I was already standing. "We'll keep them safe." I slipped the dagger he'd given me out of its sheath and flexed my fingers around it. They were still stiff and swollen, but not nearly as painful as they'd been earlier. Mae Tuck was worth thanking the Lord for, indeed.

"Let's go."

With that last whisper Bird melted into silence so complete that even the shape of him seemed less defined, less real. He flowed toward the mouth of the cave like a liquid shadow, his hunting knife in hand. I followed him, dagger at the ready, and only just spied Kent and Nell behind the lip of the cave's opening. Kent held something that looked as if it might be a chisel, which didn't surprise me; what did was the log Nell wielded over her shoulder like a club. Her gentle face was set and watchful, and silence, of course, was something she understood all too well.

I knew somehow that it was me, not Bird, they'd look to for a signal. I slowly leaned around the edge of the cave's entrance, holding my breath. For some reason I thought of how I'd held my breath as my mare jumped at the last Hunt Ball.

*Just don't be John,* I begged of the darkness. *Don't be John or his friends. Be anyone but them.*

Without the light of the fire I could hardly see. What

little light there was came from the faint luminescence of the moss growing on the small, gnarled witchwood trees.

Strange as it seemed, I could smell them before I saw them. I'd grown so used to the scents of the forest, the vivacity of green growing things and running water and rotting leaves, that the new scent was almost an assault. I remembered the stagnant, rank air in the Woodshire Village prison; this was nothing in strength to that, but it had the same sour tang.

Unwashed men, for certain; and several of them.

I took my first step outside the cave, beckoning cautiously behind me so that Bird, Kent, and Nell would follow, but only slowly.

*Just don't be John.* My heart was thumping in my ears and waking up the pain in my hands again.

*Where are they?* I thought, trying to follow my nose.

And then I stepped on one.

"Aie!"

I jumped backward, colliding with Bird. The man I hadn't seen stood up slowly, groggily, revealing a burly stature and a face darkened with a thicket of black beard—or at least, it looked black in the darkness my eyes were slowly adjusting to. I brought my dagger quickly to his neck.

He rubbed his face. All around the cave entrance other men were grumbling, pulling themselves to their feet . . .

They'd been sleeping.

"What are you doing?" I asked, my voice a croak; it was too much to hope that it would stay as strong as it had when Kent and Nell and Nellie had appeared at the cave door just the day before.

I'd thought we were so hidden, so alone. So free.

I looked closely at the bearded face before me, and then around at the men in the clearing. None of them looked like John's friends. They wore ragged clothes, and their faces were lined and rough; they showed years of hardship, even the younger ones. No noblemen these, no rich merchants' sons of the kind John would deign to associate with.

I breathed deep with relief. Still, I thought I knew them . . .

Just as I had the thought, I heard Bird's surprised murmur. "Simon!" he said. I looked over, keeping my knife to the bearded man's throat, and watched as Bird sheathed his own knife and held out his hand to the man he stood over, to help him up.

"Simon, from . . . from the jail?" I looked down at the bearded man, and my fuzzy sense of memory locked into place.

He had been one of the prisoners there. I stared.

The man stared back, waiting patiently, still showing me his palms.

I took a few more deep, slow breaths, and I retreated a step. Unlike Bird, though, I kept my knife in my hand.

"I need you to explain what you're doing here," I said. "Waiting to take us at first light, is it? Has my brother put out some reward now, for bringing me home?" I began to feel sick at the thought.

"Mistress," said another man, a younger one, without rising from his place on the ground. "We've come here to join your cause. To follow the forest's queen, for our old king's shown us no justice."

I let my eyes flutter closed for a moment, but that made me feel so tired that I immediately forced them open again.

I'd run away. That was my cause. There was another girl who'd needed to run away, too, and we'd helped each other, and Bird had come because . . . well, because he was Bird. And when Little Jane needed more help than he and I could give, we'd found someone else to help her; and with the Masons, it was really more of the same. Only more people who needed to run away, needed to hide for a while; and that it was my brother they needed to hide from endeared them to me. I didn't have a cause.

But looking at these rough men, who were breathing fresh air, walking on earth, for the first time since they'd entered Woodshire's jail . . .

I couldn't tell them that they'd come for a cause that didn't exist.

I resheathed my knife, and like Bird I offered my hand. He gave me a bow instead, and I was glad when I remembered my injuries. I flexed them again, feeling a few new cracks where the blisters had begun to dry out in the night. It was strange, how quickly and how often one could forget physical pain . . .

"If you need refuge, then you're welcome here," I said, "but don't think I'm — building an army, or rising against my brother, or anything like that. We've been making a safe place here for those who need it. That's all. In fact —" I smiled, realizing just how useful this band of rogues would be. "In fact, you can help us with the making."

❧ ❧

I couldn't bear to get back into my hammock again that night; the tight fabric around my limbs no longer felt like an enveloping hand, but rather too much like the sheets that had bound me to that huge canopied bed in my dreams.

So I sat the night out, keeping watch, just in case . . . I didn't know what. I believed they were here for the reasons they'd said, but I kept thinking of Little Jane inside the cave, of how recently she'd been hurt by a strange man — and when images of what she must have suffered pushed their way into my mind, wasn't I sure it had happened in some quiet and secluded place, and that the man who'd raped her had been as huge and burly and rough as some of these men were?

Looking around at them, most of whom had gone back to sleep almost at once when our little interview was over, I felt almost ashamed to think it.

But I stayed up and kept vigil over the cave entrance nonetheless. Little Jane would be safe and peacefully asleep as long as I had it in me to keep her that way

Bird and the Masons went back inside, and I soon heard the rumble of Nell's snore. I wrapped my cloak around my shoulders and settled into the idea of passing the rest of the night alone and wakeful.

But after a while, Bird joined me. He brought a cup of smoky just-brewed tea and pressed it into my hands, then sat down next to me on the ground, leaning back against the tree where I knelt.

He said nothing; nor did I. When I'd finished my tea I leaned against his shoulder, and he tilted his head so it rested against mine.

*You're safe now, too,* something inside me whispered. *You're safe enough to sleep.* I yawned, nestling myself closer to Bird, and my hand slipped into his. He ran his callused thumb over my bandages. I remembered the day before, the kiss that wasn't a kiss.

But for Little Jane's sake I had vowed not to sleep for the rest of the night. I pulled away from Bird and scooted a good foot away along the ground. "Thanks for the tea," I said as I straightened my spine, to take the sting out of it. He shook his head and turned away from me.

❧ ❧

In the gray light of dawn, I saw that there were even more men in the clearing than I'd thought: at least two dozen. It had to be . . .

"Every prisoner at the Woodshire Jail," said Simon, watching me count them; he and Bird had been making breakfast. "They were right apologetic about it when they tied me up, but I told them I was damned if they'd leave me to the young master's tender mercies . . . begging your pardon, mistress. I told them if they weren't going to kill me that I might as well break out with them, and live as an outlaw myself. Better than what's waiting for me when the young master sees this—meaning you no offense, mistress."

I leapt off the ground, my cloak swirling around me. "For the Lord's sake, stop calling me mistress!" I said. "Where are my fine clothes, my white horses, my dancing shoes, out here in the forest? I eat around the fire, I wash my clothes in the stream and hang them on the brambles to dry, I tear my hands to shreds, I hunt my own food . . . How many times must I say it?"

Sitting cross-legged at the cave entrance, Simon looked

as if he'd just been blown over by a strong wind. Beside him, Bird was hiding laughter behind his wooden cup.

"In fairness, Silvie, it's the first time you've said it to this lad here," Bird told me, grinning, "although I'll guess it's the last time you have to say it to anyone, now."

I didn't know what he meant until I saw him looking around the clearing, but when I followed his gaze I realized that all the men were awake, sitting up and blinking and obviously having listened to the little rant I'd just delivered.

I could have been embarrassed, but I didn't have the patience for it. "You're welcome in Woodshire Forest, gentlemen," I said. "Please call me Silvie."

# ELEVEN

# The Robbing of Loughsley

I stepped off the branch, holding my breath. I let all my weight slowly come down on my right foot. Every muscle in my body was quivering, tense.

The floor of the tree house held.

I laughed and bounded across it into Mae Tuck's arms. "It's done!" I cried.

The Mae hugged me tight, and I hugged her back, my at-long-last callused hands catching on her wimple.

"A new home for all of us," she said, "the Lady and Lord be praised."

I looked around the small room I'd entered, at the puddle of golden forest light coming in the door, and I smelled the warm honey smell of hewn wood all around us. This was one of seven similar tree house rooms, built in a cluster that spread over the sturdy branches of the three biggest trees near the cave. There were several open platforms too, in between, and from them we could look down and have a clear view of the ground without revealing our presence.

Even in winter, there were enough evergreens and ivies to keep us partly concealed. One could cross from room to room and even shoot a bow from the platforms; that seemed like a miracle to me.

I heard a noise behind me and turned to see Little Jane, smiling with pride as she surveyed the product of her direction and design.

"Well, it's your first time up here, Miss Carpenter," I said. "Did we do your ideas justice?"

My voice was light, for I knew we'd done well. But Little Jane blushed and ducked her head.

"Of course you did, Silvie," she said. "Everyone did . . . oh, wonderful work. Everyone should be proud."

"How could we not, with such a teacher?"

But that just made her blush more. "Everyone should be proud," she repeated.

That included her, I wanted to say, but I could see she didn't want to be praised.

I led her back outside, where eight or nine of the rogues, as I'd fondly come to think of them, were reclining on one platform, talking and laughing with each other. Bird was there, too, sitting a little ways apart on an overhanging branch—and so was Nellie, sitting quite close to him. Seraph glowered at them from a branch nearby, I was pleased to see.

I lectured myself not to bristle.

"Ah, Silvie," said Will Stutely, the bearded man I'd confronted the night his band arrived. "We were waiting for you and the Mae, and our carpenter. Now, those of us up here are all for another day's hard work"—the men chuckled—"but the lazybones on the ground say it's time to, ah, celebrate our accomplishment. Hey, lads?"

His deep voice carried, and an answering whoop came from below us.

"Asides which, any new home needs a blessing to warm it up, as any clergywoman worth her salt will know." He nodded to Mae Tuck, who stood just behind me.

"Oh yes," said the Mae, very seriously. "And a happy gathering is the very best sort of blessing. Especially"—her eyes were twinkling—"if there's ale."

The whoops sounded below again, louder still.

I stretched my arms above my head, smiling. "I certainly agree, and I'd be delighted not to wield a hammer for a day, too. We've all earned the right to celebrate." I ran through our remaining stores in my mind, wondering what we could most easily spare. The men certainly did their share of hunting, and they gathered tubers and late apples and greens for us too, but with so many mouths to feed, we were barely getting by.

"Right!" said Stutely. "It's settled, then." He leaned over the edge of the platform. "We're off to the pub, my lads!"

I felt my face pale with embarrassingly prim horror. I

stepped back and elbowed Little Jane. "Have you ever *been* to a public house?" I asked her.

She laughed, but the laugh was as nervous as I felt. "I've never even heard of one that lets women inside," she said. "Leastways, not women who aren't . . ." She trailed off.

I nodded sagely. "Ladies of ill repute," I said. "Ladies of pleasure."

Mae Tuck's laugh boomed out. "And what are we?" she asked, clapping both of us on the back. "Each one of us is reputed ill these days—outlaws, to be frank. And as for pleasure, we've plenty of that out here, haven't we, girls?"

I looked down at my callused hands, and I felt the tired, wholesome ache in my arms, the ache that came from helping to build houses that, the Lord and Lady willing, would keep us all sheltered for who knew how many months or years to come. I thought of the feeling my days had now, busy and sometimes worried, but still freer and more joyful than any of the plush, rigid days I'd spent at Loughsley. I thought of roast dinners by the fire, cups of tea at all hours of the day, the heartrending freshness of the forest air in morning. The comfort and freedom I'd felt the first night out here, with Bird sleeping by my side and all the restrictions of my old world fallen away.

Ill repute and pleasure.

I smiled at Mae Tuck. "Indeed," I said. "Well, girls, we're off to the public house."

"It jumps!"

The rogues broke out laughing. I wiped the ale's foam from my lips, embarrassed, but I had to laugh with them.

Even Little Jane was laughing, but I was glad to see that. In the pub where Mae Tuck had brought us, a homely place called the Rose and Chestnut in some little village I'd never heard of, we were all feeling free and happy. "Haven't you ever had ale before?" she asked.

I shook my head. "I've drunk brandy, on the hunts, or in the dead of winter after a day of skating on the frozen lake, when the blood needs warming up, and Mae Tuck's bramble wine of course is delicious," I was babbling. "But I've never had a drink that fizzes and pops in the mouth like this one."

"Never had ale!" She shook her head. "Not even when the water's bad?"

I frowned. "What do you mean?"

"Ah, you know, when something gets drowned in the well, or someone buries their house-leavings too close to the stream . . ." She trailed off. "Of course, at the big house there's always good water. Never mind. Do you like the ale, then? And what's brandy like? I've always imagined it sweet as honey."

I leaned in and winked at her conspiratorially. "I'll find us a bottle, next supply run to Loughsley. And . . . this is bitter, but it's not bad. I like the bubbles." I took another swig to check, making sure this time that I left a stripe of white foam on my lips, and I made a face at Little Jane with my new mustache.

She giggled, then clamped a hand over her mouth; but I could still see the mirth in her eyes. It brought me such joy to make her laugh.

It was only when we turned back to the rest of the table that I realized I'd thought of stealing from Loughsley again as a matter of course.

Not stealing. Taking what was mine—

No. What was ours.

The rogues were talking, I was surprised to hear, of the prince's courting voyage.

"Where on earth does he think he'll find a lass good enough for him, if not in Esting?" grumbled Stutely, pausing to quickly drain half his flagon. "The most beautiful women in the world are right here. You ask me, the royals forgot that truth much too long ago."

It was true that Prince Rioch wasn't the first to seek a spouse abroad; the royal family, and the nobles rich enough to follow their example, had been marrying from outside Esting's borders as long as anyone could remember. The practice helped maintain diplomatic relations, of course, but it was also one of the reasons it was so easy to tell peasants and royalty apart on sight: Esting's commoners were somewhat fair, with hair that was brown or reddish or blond. Nobles were generally either dark-skinned, with curling black hair and long, thick lashes like the people of the Sudlands, or icy-pale with colorless eyes and the feathery white hair of Nordsk's snowbound inhabitants.

Indeed, while my own hair was dark blond and only slightly curled, my skin was darker than that of anyone else at the table: an inheritance from a grandmother who had been a Su duchess. I'd always been taught to value it as a sign of my own nobility. But here, did it only make me conspicuous? I glanced around the pub, suddenly nervous, pulling my sleeves farther down over my wrists.

Bird, on my other side, shook his head. "Don't worry." He nodded toward a back corner of the bar. Following his gaze, I spotted a woman—one of the ladies of pleasure I'd spoken of with Little Jane and the Mae back in the forest— flirting with a tall, skinny man; she had feathery, near-white hair and gray eyes, and the expanse of bosom displayed by her tight bodice was certainly very pale. "Plenty of folks with exotic looks around every place," he said. "Bastards, of course, and very impolite to mention it to them. No one will think you're an actual noble—just an unclaimed child of one."

I felt naive again, and foolish enough that I didn't even blink at Bird's rough language. What he said made sense, of course.

But I shook my head to settle my hood lower over my forehead, to shadow my dark, long-lashed eyes.

"Is there no wrong we haven't done?" I said suddenly, impatiently, slapping my empty mug down on the table.

Bird leaned forward. "Silvie, I didn't mean—"

"Little Jane, how often was the water bad, in the village?" My voice was fierce, hard. I'd stood up from the table without realizing.

Little Jane looked up at me, cautious. "Why, a few times a year."

"And people at Loughsley knew about this? John? My . . . my father?" I hated even to say their names together that way, but I had to know.

Little Jane shrugged. "They were told. But the big house water could never be spared."

I thought of my father's walled gardens, full of plants from all over the three continents, lush and verdant. I thought of how I'd loved them, without ever bothering to think of where the water that sustained them came from, or what good it might do elsewhere. I thought of the man-made waterfall by the pomegranate trees, where I used to swim in summer—with a calm river not half a mile away. And a whole village going without clean water, not far beyond that.

People were looking at me now indeed; all over the pub they were staring. Even the feathery-haired woman had turned around in her customer's lap, and she regarded me with wary amusement even while the man kept kissing her shoulder.

I lowered my voice and placed my hands on the table. "We're going back to Loughsley tonight," I said, running my finger along the seam between two slats of wood as if I were tracing a path. "And this time we'll take more than food."

❧ ❧

Loughsley Abbey floated over the water like a ghost, but I was the one haunting it.

I stole in through the back garden gate, the same way I'd left with Bird after the Hunt Ball, when we were just going for a walk. For some reason, our leaving for good later that night didn't loom nearly so large in my mind. I felt more and more in my heart as though I'd truly left when I'd fled from the ball, from Lord Danton, from John and the way he looked at me.

I'd abandoned my home in my heart even then.

I crept through the gardens in my sturdy hunting boots, remembering how quickly the dew and lake water had soaked through my dancing shoes. I never took dry feet for granted now. How much had I changed in just a few months?

How much would I change as the year, or the years, wore on?

I stopped, my head buzzing. I leaned over with my

hands on my thighs, and it didn't feel as if I could breathe deeply enough to steady myself again. The ground below me started to pop and fizz like the ale in the pub. I felt the breaths I was trying to take turn to gasps, then wheezes.

My hands went slick and cold and they slipped off the front of my skirt. I stumbled forward, still gasping—

But before I hit the ground, Bird and Little Jane both caught me.

"Steady," Bird murmured, not an instruction but a naming, an invocation; and I found what he called up in me.

"You all right, Silvie?" Little Jane asked.

I could feel the steadiness Bird had named coming out in the smile I gave her. "Don't worry about me," I said. "I'm not the one carrying a passenger. You've more right to faint than I do."

She smirked and looked at the ground, then gave my arm a squeeze that I thought might leave bruises.

"Right," I said briskly. "Everyone sure of their plans?"

They nodded silently and let me go. Around them the rogues, the Masons, and Mae Tuck nodded too.

"Good. We'll meet back here in no more than three hours."

Bird and Little Jane turned toward the Abbey's stable yard, the others found their paths, and I made my way to what had been my own balcony.

❧ ❧

The smooth, twisting ivy made good purchase for my hands and feet, but it was hard to keep a firm enough grip on the slippery bark to pull myself up. I'd climbed down from this balcony so many times that I thought climbing up would be easy—and how many trees had I climbed, all my life and especially in these last few weeks?

By the time I made it up to the balustrade and clambered my way over, I was sweating and my muscles burned. I was hungry enough to forget my jewelry box and go straight for the bowl of wrapped sweetmeats that always sat on my bureau.

The first bite was so sugary it made my eyes water. I coughed and swallowed immediately; I hadn't had food so rich or strong in weeks, and though I'd always loved sweets, my tongue seemed to be telling me it didn't like the taste.

I scowled and opened another candy, forcing myself to chew it slowly, and then I emptied the rest of the bowl into my satchel. The wrappings crinkled against each other like leaves as they tumbled in. The sugar would do almost as much as the fire to keep us warm as the winter set in, at least while it lasted. I wished I'd remembered to tell Bird to take the rest of the confections from the kitchen, for neither my father nor John fancied sweets, and they wouldn't be missed.

How had I taken such food for granted, so short a time ago? How had I smiled at the soft fullness of my limbs and hips and belly only because I knew they were beautiful, and not because they meant I was well fed?

I heard a muffled sound behind me.

I froze, still holding the bowl over my open bag.

Someone was sleeping in my bed.

❧ ❧

I stepped closer, not allowing myself to shake. All I could think of, somehow, was an old nursery story: Psyche, the girl who believed she'd married a monster. When she finally raised her candle to look at the bridegroom in bed with her, she saw an angel instead, the most beautiful man in the world.

I didn't expect an angel.

I didn't think I'd see a monster, either, but John's face against my pillow made me startle backward with as much revulsion as if I had.

My brother snored lightly, and he frowned a little in his sleep. He kept as tight a grip on the pillow as he always kept on his horse's reins, and it made me wonder—absurd thought—when I'd ever seen his hands relaxed, rather than clenched into fists.

Maybe I never had.

My loose hair fell forward and brushed his cheek.

His frown deepened, his hand grew tighter on the

pillow, and he groaned. It was a sound of such quiet long-ing, and it made me more afraid than I could remember being since I was a little girl . . . no, since I had seen in his face the impossibility of the life he'd chosen for me at the Hunt Ball. The impossibility that had changed my life.

I strode quickly and silently back to my bureau, my spine iron, and I tucked my whole jewelry box into the satchel. I told myself I'd bring back the heirlooms someday, the things of my mother's that my father would miss. But I couldn't bear to sort through them now, if it meant staying in my bedroom with my brother even one more instant. Breathing the same air that he breathed.

Before I ran away to the forest, I'd been used to him, somehow, how it felt to be near him, to live in the house where he lived. Still, I'd known . . . something, some wrongness; it was part of what had made me so willing, so eager, to run.

It had taken me only a few months to forget the taste of sweetmeats. It had taken even less time to forget the weight, the burden, of the fear I carried in this house. The fear I —

I still couldn't name it, couldn't face it. Not now. I had my jewelry, and I knew where to find the other valuables in the house. I loosed my hold over my body and let myself flee.

I was halfway down the balcony wall again before I re-membered the one last thing I'd wanted to do. I felt sick at the mere thought of going back to my bedroom, but I'd feel sicker tomorrow, and who knew for how long after, if I didn't do this one thing more.

I ran across the garden and set down my heavy satchel in the seat of Bird's secret chair. I looked up at the moon, at the surrounding sky; I thought I had plenty of time left, but I couldn't be sure.

I turned back and ran again toward Loughsley Abbey.

❦ ❦

I refused to worry too much about my father's room being empty. John didn't seem to have booted him from the master suite, at least; his robe still hung in its place by the door, and the toilet table held a half-empty bottle of the Su cologne he'd always favored.

The bedclothes were rumpled. When I placed a cautious hand on the pillow, it was cold.

The first place I looked for him, naturally, was the library. Any time either of us couldn't sleep, or didn't wish to, it was the first place we would go. If we happened to meet each other there, Father would smile and ring the bell, and a yawning servant would bring us tea, a pipe (for him), and biscuits (for me). How many nights we'd spent reading in companionable silence, the fire stoked for us before the servant left.

My memories focused on the servant now, as I stood in

the dark and cold library. How tired she must have been, called out of bed in the middle of the night after a long day's work to indulge our whims. How I had never, even once, thought about that before—or if I had, it hadn't bothered me.

What else had I never bothered to see?

In the shadows, something stirred. Slowly.

"Father," I murmured, rushing to embrace him.

His back was thin and frail, and even through his night-shirt it felt cold. He'd been sitting in one of the wingback chairs by the fireplace, so still—so still in the dark, and so diminished and thin, that I hadn't even seen he was there. I hadn't noticed him at all.

I pulled the thick sheepskin from where it hung over the back of the chair and draped it around his back. "You've forgotten your robe, Father," I said. "I'll call someone to—I'll get it for you." When I pressed one of his hands in both of mine, it was cold too, cold as stone, cold as night. It felt shockingly light. There was no weight, no strength in it at all.

"Kind of you, dear," he said, shifting his shoulders to settle the wool around them. "It's a trifle cool in here."

I dropped his hand, then touched it again at once. "I've missed you, Father," I said quietly. "I'm so—I'm so sorry. I had to leave."

He shook his head. "I always knew you'd come back. I

finished your bridge, you know. In the morning we'll go look at it, when it's warmer and light. You mustn't catch a chill." I flinched, remembering my mother shivering in her bed.

The Wedding-Ring Bridge, my mother's bridge. It wasn't, as I'd dared to hope, as I'd dared to comfort myself when I couldn't sleep in the cave at night, that he was just far gone enough not to know that I'd left. He was worse than that. He didn't even know me; he thought I was my mother.

But this left open such an evil temptation that I could not resist it. If he thought I was my mother, I could learn the things he'd tell only her.

"How are the children? Have they grown up well?" I couldn't quite bear to call him by his first name.

"John is a good boy. He looks after everything, ever since I got sick . . . He's the real lord of Loughsley now. He has my judgment in everything. A firm hand." My father smiled vacantly.

It took more will than I'd thought not to say anything. But what good would it do to deprive my father of the comfort he took from his belief in John's goodness, his faith in his son's?

"But Silviana . . . Darling, I am . . . I am ashamed to tell you."

I steeled every part of myself. "Tell me."

"Silviana ran away with a servant boy, because she didn't

love us." This voice rang out strong and clear behind me, and I wheeled to face it. "Silviana threw away her virtue. She has no proper family feeling. I am so sorry to tell you, Mother, but your only daughter hates us all."

John was advancing on me with every word. Wearing only his nightclothes, he reminded me of Father at the Hunt Ball, and the two of them merged, images rippling in a pool inside my mind, until the faces of the father I loved and the brother I feared did truly seem one and the same.

Was it John or my father who walked toward me, or whose cold hand I held? Which woman was trapped in Loughsley Abbey, and which one lay free in the cold earth at the base of the oak tree by the Wedding-Ring Bridge? Was I myself or my mother? Myself or—

My hands were clenched tight and starting to ache. I felt their strength and warmth, their rough calluses. I felt my father's cold hand in mine and I let it go. I felt the firm set of my feet on the plush Nordsk carpet that lay on the library floor.

I felt my skin, every inch of it. John touching none. He'd stepped close to me, but then he'd stopped. He wasn't even reaching out.

"But if she's come back," he said, his voice soft and gentle, "perhaps it means she's repented. Perhaps it means she loves us after all."

John wasn't touching any part of me, wasn't holding me there. He never had. I had always been free to go.

So I turned and ran out the library's far archway.

I didn't even register most of the rooms I fled through. When I came to the dining room, I snatched up one of the gold candelabras on the table. I meant to take another, but the first was so heavy I staggered from its weight, even with the new strength I'd gained from building tree houses.

"Silviana!" John was closer behind me than I realized. He caught me around the waist and pulled me upright. "Silviana, here, let me help you . . ."

That same longing was in his voice that I'd heard when he'd groaned in his sleep, in my bed. The gentleness, the hesitation in his hands when he touched me, when I knew just how violent a man he really was. For all the softness in his grip, I knew how close and hard he wanted to hold me.

I lifted the heavy gold candelabra and hit him across the temple.

He fell to the floor, limp, and I kept running.

I was the last one to return to the Wedding-Ring Bridge. I was cheered like a hero as I turned around the bend in the river's edge, and for a moment, I felt like one, too.

Will Stutely took the candelabra I handed to him and whistled at its weight. I saw him stare for a moment at the blood on its base, but he said nothing; his eyes only flickered over me for a moment, as if to make sure that the blood wasn't mine, and then he tucked it into the large sack he and the rogues had brought back from the treasury.

"The spare key was just where you told us it'd be, Silvie," he said.

To be Silvie again, and not Silviana, was a relief. To cross the bridge into Woodshire Village and then to move on toward the enveloping arms of the forest in the predawn gray light, even more so. We left three coins at each door that we passed, enough to pay the raise in the sheriff's taxes or to buy food for winter, if they'd paid their taxes already in produce. Enough to keep them going, and more than enough left over to feed our growing band.

We could melt down the candelabra and those pieces of my jewelry that were too identifiable to pawn. After my encounter with my father and John I didn't feel the least need to give any of it back anymore, not even my mother's things. I knew they were going where they would be needed.

I could see the glow of Bird's banked, still-burning fire as soon as we entered the clearing. The air was changing, the sky growing paler.

I felt something brush my face, like a small feather. It reminded me of Scarlet, but she was in her nest with Much. I touched my face and a melting droplet came away on my finger: snow.

Winter had come, but there was gold in our hands and fire in our hearth. Better still, we'd given that security to everyone in Woodshire Village.

Bird was already setting a kettle to boil and stoking the fire. I hurried into the cave to join him, trying not to think about whether I'd killed my brother.

*Winter*

# *Interlude*

D ead of winter, frozen rivers. White threads through the forest, white tangles on a green loom. A scrim of frost on every fallen leaf.

Snow collects around Loughsley Abbey, even when it melts away from other places. The masses of rock and shadow in the cliffs hold on to cold.

Inside the house we would eat wild venison, rich candies, bread baked from taxed grain, and drink mulled wine and hot brandy from realms abroad that cost as much by the cup, I later learned, as would buy a family food for a month in the village.

In the village they wrapped their feet in flannel so their toes wouldn't blacken with frostbite. In the village we took so much in taxes that one or two small children would always starve before the spring. We took more than we needed to give to the king, who took more than he needed, too.

And we used it to buy mulled wine.

I didn't know then, but I know it now.

We might as well have been drinking their blood.

# ~ TWELVE ~

# *Anna Robin*

A red silk purse sailed over my head. It was small, and in my old life I wouldn't have looked twice at it. But the gold inside was a year's rent for a Woodshire smallholder, someone who couldn't abandon his crops or stock or mill to join our refuge in the forest, Kent Mason had said when he saw it. A whole year's rent, a whole year of shelter, and a whole year of keeping the crops and animals someone needed to feed his own children.

The purse sailed back and forth through the air like a magic trick, like a children's game, tossed from one pair of hands to another as we tramped toward the village to deliver it.

Stutely made a leap and caught it in midair, then swung it around his finger on its silk string. He was laughing and grinning like everyone else, but as we approached the river, with the miller's cottage across a tiny stone bridge, his face grew somber. The rogues hung back, and after a moment I realized that they were all looking at me.

"Best for you to give it to them, Silvie," said Kent, next to me. Nell, beside him, nodded.

"But—" I looked at the tiny cottage, at the old and patched-together but freshly whitewashed mill stuck in the frozen stream. "I don't want it to look like pity, coming from me," I said. "Like—like patronage."

"Afraid of not giving us credit? Isn't the lass too kind?" Even when he was trying to be serious, Stutely's good humor shone; his bright blue eyes twinkled over his dark beard as he raised his eyebrows at me. "What, you'd rather it look like thievery?"

I snatched the purse from his hand. "Just don't want them to get any kind ideas about us nobles, is all," I said, dropping into my most formal curtsey. But Stutely had brought out my stubbornness, just as he'd meant to, and as the rogues smothered their laughter I marched toward the door.

It was true, though, that I didn't want these people to think *I* was giving them gold, out of some naive, kindhearted impulse—especially when my own brother would arrive any day to take that gold back.

My blow hadn't killed him, that night at Loughsley. I'd learned that soon enough, when Bird's falcon had brought a "Wanted, Alive" notice with my name on it back to the forest. A warning from Bird's mother—with *congratulations* scrawled on the reverse of the paper.

Seeing the reward my brother offered for my capture wasn't a shock. Long before I'd struck him with the candelabra, before I'd vowed in the pub to take back what he and my family had stolen, before I'd run to the forest with Little Jane and Bird or even shot the prince's wounded hart—long before then, I had known deep inside that he'd capture me if he could. Everything I'd done in the past few months had just given him an excuse.

I looked at the purse in my hand. I was still showing him just how free I was.

So I pulled my hood low over my forehead, a motion that had grown to almost a habit by then, and I drew my scarf over my mouth, and I simply tucked the purse behind a rock that lay to the side of the door. Whoever opened the door would see the bright silk there, but no one would spy it coming in.

It was almost dark, and I thought we'd get away undetected. But as I turned to walk back, I saw someone staring out at me through the cottage window: a small face, a red-haired child barely out of babyhood. Her eyes were as wide as if she'd just seen a spirit, and they locked with mine for a moment, each of us caught in the other's gaze.

Then the little girl vanished. I knew she'd be running to tell her parents there was someone outside.

I walked as quickly as I could across the bridge without

slipping in the snow. "Come on!" I told the group, and we were moving back to the road and toward our forest home in moments.

Everyone was smiling and laughing, and there was a buzz of energy in the air, a feeling I'd come to know well in the last month.

This one had been a highway robbery, holding up a gilded Brethren carriage that seemed to mock the very idea of vows of poverty. I knew Mae Tuck would be delighted by our choice of victim — but the thrill we all felt didn't come from knowing we were bringing money to someone who needed it, or that we'd stolen from someone who neither needed nor deserved what they had.

No; it was the stealing itself, the act of it, the cleverness and coordination of what we'd done together. We had executed the thievery perfectly, with all the grace of a waltz. The soft, complacent Brethren in the carriage never stood a chance.

It was the same feeling that I used to get from dancing, in fact, or from jumping a good horse. The rush of coming together with someone else to do something elegant, something beautiful, that I could never have done alone.

It had nothing to do with virtue at all.

As we moved off the road and into the forest, the sound of the frost under our feet changed from a quiet murmur to a crunch like the gnashing of teeth. Very little snow had made its way through the branches to the forest floor, not all winter, even though we were now a few weeks into the new year. But that same cover meant that the sun never shone through enough to melt the frost, either. Even at noon it dusted the leaves on the ground like fine sugar.

I heard a familiar caw overhead. Bird's falcon plunged out of the canopy and circled just a few feet above our heads—above my head, in particular. She called again, and then again.

"Stop a moment," I told the group.

I knew whom she was calling for, and I squinted into the growing darkness of the forest ahead, trying to find her master in the gloom. For a few minutes I could see nothing. Then Bird emerged from above as well, climbing down the trunk of a beech tree ten yards or so away from us. During our months in the forest he'd honed our childhood knack for moving faster over the network of branches in the canopy than dodging between trees on the ground.

"Bird, what are you doing?" I asked as he came toward me. He was breathing heavily, and as I got closer I could see that he looked—not scared exactly, but . . . "I thought we agreed you'd stay behind with Little Jane and the Mae this time, in case—"

"Yes. In case, yes. In case is happening." He was close enough to me now that I could see that his color was high.

He seemed to have trouble getting even those disjointed words out.

"Bird?"

Seraph alighted on his arm and gave his ear a firm nip. As clearly as if she'd spoken, she was telling him to calm down.

He took a long, shuddering breath. "You're right, my lass. Thanks." He looked at me, his eyes bright. "She asked me to come see if I could find you. She said not to worry, the Mae has her well in hand, but . . . Silvie. Silvie, Little Jane's baby is coming, right now."

"I thought she had another two weeks," I whispered. An excited murmur rose around us, but I barely heard it. How I had hoped to be there, to hold her hand . . .

Perhaps it wasn't too late. "We'll be quicker up in the trees," I said to Bird, and he nodded. I turned to the group. "You'll find your way back all right?"

Stutely laughed. "Of course we will," he said. "Can't swing through the trees like the pair of you, but we'll still return in time to hear the wee thing's first holler, I'd say. Go on, go to your friend."

Kent stepped past Stutely, his face worried and happy at once. "Bring her all our luck," he said, "and all our love."

Everyone echoed his wishes, but I was already up in the branches with Bird, and flying toward home.

❧ ❧

"In the cave, so they'd have the fire," Bird told me as we stepped, heaving, onto the platform at the edge of the miniature village of tree houses that Little Jane had shown us how to build.

But he didn't need to say. I could hear them.

I'd expected screaming, sharp cries; not from the baby, but from Little Jane. But the sounds I heard, while loud, were not sharp. Instead, there was a low moan, then a pause, long enough for me to realize that I feared silence more than any scream, any noise, because noise meant breath and life. And then another deep, guttural sound, a sound that seemed more as if it might have come from the mouth of the cave itself than from a human throat.

In the few moments it had taken to listen to those two moans I had climbed down to earth again and hurried through the clearing.

I crossed the threshold of the cave. My heart was pounding so hard I could feel it in my fingertips.

But Little Jane would need me to be calm. I remembered Bird's falcon biting his ear and I forced myself to breathe slowly, to feel the air around me, the solid floor of the cave under my feet, the heat of the fire. I made myself stop trembling as I looked around.

Little Jane groaned again. She was leaning on her hammock. She wore only her shift, and it was hiked up over her hips. Her bare legs glowed pale where the firelight touched them. Her eyes were closed, and she rocked back and forth as she moaned. Her hands clutched the fabric of the hammock so hard that her knuckles were white.

Mae Tuck stood behind her, as calm and unassuming as ever, leaning hard on Little Jane's lower back with her palms, putting all the strength she had into her task. "This one's nearly over," she said. "Good girl."

I realized I'd been standing as still as a statue. "I'm here, Little Jane," I said, walking toward her. "I'm here."

Her eyes didn't open; I didn't think she'd even heard me. She just kept rocking, letting out that long, slow moan.

But Mae Tuck looked up at me and smiled. "Ah, Silvie," she said. "You might take this over, would you? You've good strong arms, and I want to stir the tisane for the linens."

I came forward, my hands already extended. "Just as we practiced, right?"

Mae Tuck nodded and drew away.

Little Jane grew quiet, and she turned toward me, her eyes slowly opening. "Silvie," she said, her voice a whisper. "I'm glad you're here, Silvie." It was as if she was speaking to me from somewhere deep inside herself, some country I'd never visited.

I smoothed a strand of hair that sweat had pasted to her forehead. "I wanted to be here," I said. "Of course I did."

She nodded. Her eyes started to flutter closed again, and this time when she spoke she sounded even farther away.

"She's glad, too," she said. "She wants to meet—" Her voice cut off; every part of her face grew still and stubborn and tense.

I put my hands on her back the way Mae Tuck had shown me and I pressed down hard. Little Jane leaned forward, putting all her weight on the hammock, and I put all my weight onto her back. This time when she moaned I could feel the sound vibrate through both our bodies. I felt her change under my hands, every muscle in her torso grow hard, and even from behind I could see her wide belly lift and tighten as it tensed.

I didn't know how much time passed after that. I kept pushing against her when she needed me. Eventually each wave of pain would leave her, and she would quiet and her eyes would open. When she tired of leaning against the hammock we paced the cave together, around and around the fire, the Mae coming to us every few minutes to check on Little Jane's progression. Keep walking, she said; stay upright as long as you can. Lean on Silvie if you want to; lean on me.

And she did. It hurt to watch her, to witness such pain. I would have shared it with her, if I could, and I reminded myself of that every time my arms began to ache from pressing on her back, or my legs to cramp from helping to hold her up. Anything I felt then, any pain I'd ever felt in my life,

I thought, was just a drop in the ocean of what Little Jane felt that night.

She moaned and paced, and she wept. Her body, big as it was, seemed small compared to the force of what moved in and through her.

Yet I wasn't frightened for her: I saw such strength, such stubbornness, in the way she responded to each cycle of pain. When she stopped and looked at me and said, in as clear and present a voice as she'd yet used, "I can't do it, Silvie," I knew beyond doubt that she was wrong.

"You can," I said, shifting my weight so I could take yet more of hers. "You're doing it already. You carried this baby in the forest all these months. We made a life here, a life that is better for all of us because of you. Look at how we live now! You brought Mae Tuck to us. We would never have found her without you. And the rogues came in her wake, and oh, look at the homes you taught us to build. We're surviving the winter out here thanks to you, Little Jane. You're a mother to all of us already."

I was babbling, murmuring what might as well have been nonsense words for all the notice Little Jane took of them. She clutched her belly and dropped to kneel on the floor, her low moans breaking at last into a high, uneven keen.

"I can't, I can't," she said. Her whole body was shaking.

Mae Tuck came forward with fresh linens and nodded, not to me or Little Jane, but as if she were in conversation with the birth itself. "It's time, then," she announced.

I looked up.

"It's always nearly over when they say they can't do it."

I took a deep breath. Little Jane didn't seem to hear what Mae Tuck had said, but after a minute her keening lowered again to a moan, and a smallest fraction of the tension on her face began to lift.

"All right, child, this one's passing," the Mae said, kneeling down with her and putting her hands gently but firmly on either side of her belly. "Now, do you think you could lie on your side, so I can see how far you've come?"

Then a sound I never would have guessed I'd hear in such a moment came out of Little Jane's mouth. It was short, it was harsh—but it was laughter.

"Lie down? Don't have to tell me twice," she said.

I grabbed a folded blanket pilfered from Loughsley from a nearby stack and laid it under her head as a cushion. I offered her my hand to hold, but she shook her head. "I'm afraid I'd break your bones, with how tight I'll squeeze," she said. "Safer to grab the blanket."

"Break my bones if you like," I said. "It might feel good for you to see someone sharing the pain."

She laughed again, but it was even shorter and harsher than the last time. "The next one's coming in a moment now," she whispered. "I won't think anything's funny—Mae Tuck . . ." Her voice was fading again, her eyes closing.

"Yes, you're doing so well, child, so well," the Mae said. "Do you feel as if you want to push?"

"I'm so tired," Little Jane panted. "I don't know if I can . . . Oh, it's coming, it's coming . . ." The moan started again, from low inside her.

"You're nearly done now, child," said the Mae. "Your body knows what to do. Let it show you."

Little Jane nodded, her head on the pillow, moaning louder. She looked exhausted, her face pale and drawn, her hair soaked through with sweat, but I could see that she was pushing after all.

"Your hand, Silvie, your hand—"

I gave it. She squeezed so hard that I thought she might have been right about breaking my bones.

Little Jane grimaced and then cried out. I could see the tension, the contraction, as it left her belly. She panted a few times, then lifted her head. "It felt good to push," she told us. "It was what I wanted to do. Was I right? Is it time?"

"Yes," said the Mae. A smile was breaking out on her face. "I could see your little one's head for a minute there."

Little Jane and I both stared at her.

"Silvie," whispered Little Jane, without looking at me, "can you see my baby's head?"

"She can if she comes down here with me for the next push," the Mae said.

Little Jane nodded, closing her eyes again.

I stood up and rearranged myself so that I was kneeling next to the Mae, but I could still reach up and let Little Jane hold my hand. Mae Tuck was just replacing the linen under Little Jane's bottom with a fresh layer. There was blood and fluid, but as Jane began to push again all I could look at was the small circle, the swirl of dark hair, that began to emerge between Little Jane's legs.

Little Jane grunted and squeezed my hand to breaking, and the small delicate head pushed farther, farther, and then as Little Jane cried out at the end of that moment's strength, the baby retreated inside her again. I thought for some reason of all the rivers running through the forest, all their slick icy surfaces that seemed so still, and all the rushing dark water underneath. Rushing always, moving always, alive through all the seeming stillness of winter.

"I saw her," I told Little Jane. My voice was breaking; I felt tears on my face. "Little Jane, she's so close. She's coming."

She lifted her head from the pillow. "She's coming," she echoed. She breathed in through her nose, and I watched her jaw set with determination. "Mae Tuck, I want to get up."

The Mae nodded, and she and I put our arms under

Little Jane's to help support her as she knelt upright. "Can I lean against you, Silvie?"

"You never have to ask."

So I stood against the wall, and she leaned against me, her face against my belly, one arm wrapped around my waist; and with her other arm she reached down and helped Mae Tuck catch her own baby.

Quickly testing the baby's limbs with her practiced hands, Mae Tuck said, "You see? It's always almost over when you say you can't do it."

Little Jane sank down on the floor again, and I piled the blankets and linens behind her so she could rest, half sitting, against the cave wall. The lacing on the front of her shift had long since come undone, and Mae Tuck laid the baby on her bare chest.

The little thing wasn't crying. I looked at it in alarm, and then at the Mae. "Don't they shout, when they're born?" I asked.

She smiled, shaking her head. "Not always. Listen to the strong breath this one's making; we've got a contented little girl on our hands, that's all."

"A girl after all," I whispered.

Little Jane stroked her baby's forehead, murmuring something so quiet I couldn't hear the words. But they weren't meant for me. She was sweaty and tired, still pale; her baby was puffy and strangely purple, and streaked with red and white fluids. Mae Tuck smoothed another clean linen over the new baby and mother, to keep them warm.

All three of them glowed like paintings of saints. And Little Jane didn't look far away anymore: she had come back safely from that country where I'd never been. The presence and the power of her filled up the whole cave.

❦ ❦

After the baby had nursed and both she and Little Jane had fallen asleep, Mae Tuck nodded and turned to me. "This is their time, now," she said. "Let's give them a few hours' privacy."

I was not quite prepared for the anticipatory stillness that waited for us outside the cave. Every single member of our band stared at Mae Tuck and me eagerly, anxiously. I thought the Mae would speak, but she touched my arm and then gestured to the group, as if to say, *Go on*.

"A girl," I said, surprised to hear how hoarse my voice had gone. "And both she and Little Jane resting and well."

The cheer that went up was so loud Mae Tuck held up both her hands.

"Resting, she said! Didn't you hear?"

The cheer faded to a joyful murmur.

"What can we do to help?" Will Stutely asked, stepping forward. Behind him the rogues, tired from the day's adventures, still stood up eagerly, ready to do whatever needed doing.

"You can wash yourselves in the river, for one thing, before you even think of going near that baby," I informed him.

Mae Tuck nodded approvingly.

"The river?" Stutely gave a theatrical shiver. "It's pure ice!"

"Good," I said sweetly. "It might actually freeze the stink off you."

"What!" A white grin broke through Stutely's black beard even as he pretended to grumble. "I'm not half as smelly as Kent. Just ask his wife."

Nell Mason leaned in to sniff her husband, then recoiled with her tongue stuck out and her eyes rolling. Kent clasped his hands over his heart in mock offense.

The teasing and laughter escalated until Stutely announced that he was going to toss all of us into the river for a bath, like it or not—which resulted in Simon and Kent nodding to each other and then rushing at the tall Stutely and carrying him off.

A crackling sound of ice breaking, a big splash, and a bigger shout soon followed.

"Here," Bird said, laughing, "I'll start a new fire out here tonight. Stutely'll be glad of it in a few minutes."

"And of a blanket, if we've any to spare," I said. Mae Tuck went bustling off to retrieve one.

Before long Stutely was back, dripping. I was amused to see that Simon and Kent were just as sopping wet as he was. The rest of us helped stoke the fire Bird had started.

Stutely, Simon, and Kent huddled together near the flames, sharing a blanket and body heat, each of them wearing ill-fitting clothes — Stutely even using a red flannel petticoat that had once been mine but had become communal property as a kind of toga.

Soon we had a bonfire tall enough to lick the frost off the canopy. No fear of burning, in the depths of cold and wet January, but still we built it far from the hidden tree houses.

After we ate I went in to bring some food to Little Jane. I thought she was still sleeping, the baby resting on her chest, and I set the tin bowl down where she'd find it when she woke. But as I turned to leave, her voice stopped me.

"She's called Anna," she said. "After you."

I sank down next to her. Her face was radiant in the low light from the banked fire at the cave's entrance.

"Me? Oh, Little Jane . . ."

"Since you're using only part of your name out here, I hoped you wouldn't mind lending her the other bit." She smiled. "Her second name is Robin, after Bird, for she's a winter baby, and a robin is a winter bird." She looked up at me, and her eyes were apprehensive. "Do you mind?"

I couldn't speak. I shook my head, and I reached out reverently to touch Anna Robin's forehead.

"It's you and Bird who got us here," Little Jane went on. "You made sure I was alive to see this day. And, Silvie . . ." She swallowed, and she touched her lips to the crown of Anna's head. After a long breath in, she looked back up at me. "Anna's father . . ."

I shook my head again. "What right has he to that title?"

"None. I know. But, Silvie . . . I thought I'd never tell you, I'd never be brave enough. But I know now, how brave I am." She took a long breath. "Anna's blood to you, you see. Her father—the one who sent her coming, anyway— it was your brother." She shifted to hold her baby closer. "He has no right, and he never will. I know. But I want her to be—not your brother's daughter, but your niece."

What did I feel, in that moment? Longing that the blow I'd dealt my brother had killed him after all? Rage, hatred, vengeance?

All those were there, waiting to be felt. But as Little Jane lifted her sleeping daughter and I took my niece in my arms, love overwhelmed me, love that rushed like a warm flood through my body and soul, filling me up so that everything else was washed away.

"She has your mouth, I think," Little Jane said.

I shook my head, and a tear dropped onto Anna Robin's round cheek. No feature of mine had ever been so perfect.

Outside the rogues laughed and murmured around the bonfire. Cold and darkness surrounded us on all sides, but here in the forest, there was light and life.

Spring

# ~THIRTEEN~

# Merriment

Scarlet's talons dug into my shoulder and her wings slapped at my face as she landed. I reached up to stroke the soft feathers under her beak. She chirruped and leaned into my hand, her wide eyes fluttering closed.

"No catch for us again today, hey, my lass?" I asked her, although the answer was obvious from the lack of vermin lying at my feet.

Bird looked up from deboning the large trout Seraph had brought him just minutes earlier. "By the Lady and Lord, that creature's the worst hunter I ever trained," he said. "How old is she now, and never brought back a single catch? I don't know how she hasn't starved to death!"

Bird knew very well how Scarlet ate, and he watched me pull a strip of dried boar meat out of my pocket and offer it to the young owl, who immediately snapped it up and tilted her head so that it disappeared in one gulping, loud swallow. Scarlet hooted again and nuzzled my face. "Only a few months," I said, returning her owly embrace by pressing my own cheek against hers. "Besides, she's so affectionate."

Bird snorted. "She's just looking for more free meals. See there; she'd be fluttering her lashes, if she had any, the little rogue." But his eyes were laughing.

"Sure, don't go calling that kettle black, Falconer," said Stutely, who was walking out of the trees with a bundle of dry timber strapped to his back. "We're every one of us rogues, as our dear sheriff won't let us forget. We've got to stay friends among ourselves—it's just the owl knows that better than some. A fair community spirit, her. And Little Jane's owl's enough of a hunter for the two of them."

It was true: Much provided rabbits and fish for our fire even more often than Seraph did. Ever since Anna Robin had arrived, the young owl had seemed to decide overnight that he was a kind of feathery parent, and that the new chick in the nest, being already the size of a grown-up owl, needed enough meat to feed a small army. It was too bad he didn't seem to understand the idea of milk, or I wouldn't have put it past him to try to fly a dairy cow out to us.

"Silvie, look what I found today." Bird beckoned me over to an edge of the clearing. "Snowdrops."

I stared: in the evening gloom you could nearly mistake the tiny bells for large snowflakes, but there they were, stubbornly pushing their way out of the cold soil. If they were growing here, under the canopy, they would be practically carpeting the ground outside the forest by now. Spring had come.

❧ ❧

Our life among the trees was busier and happier than it had ever been.

There was a baby to care for, for one: looking after a tiny infant took more effort than I could have thought possible. We all helped. A tailor named Arthur who had come to us in the winter, another refugee from my brother, stitched old cotton strips into diapers for her. Will Stutely doggedly washed them in the river each day and hung them out to dry, insisting with a laugh that he was the only one who could handle the stench, used as he was to the smell of himself.

I brought Little Jane food, often feeding it to her while she nursed the baby, and I watched my niece while the young mother slept.

Little Jane had recovered well, but even with all our help, she was still exhausted, for she had to wake up every few hours to nurse. Mae Tuck told me that every time a new group joined our growing forest community, she prayed to the Lady that one among them would be a nursing mother with whom Little Jane could share the burden of night feedings.

One day in April her prayers were answered. Not a

nursing mother, but a family with two white goats in tow. The animals moved nimbly through the forest, placing their small hooves between roots and rocks with the precision of dancers.

"We didn't want to come to you empty-handed," said the elderly woman who led the goats, holding the hand of a young boy who looked simply like a child version of herself. "I know we cannot help in your ventures, for I am too old and Eric still too young"—the boy scowled, and I could see from the longing way he stared at Stutely and Bird, who were laughing as they sparred each other with blackthorn staffs in the clearing, that he disagreed with his grandmother on that score—"and we had nothing else left to bring, after the sheriff's last takings, but Nanny and Ninny. He'd have taken them, too, if Eric hadn't hidden them first."

"Well, that was very clever of you," I said to the boy, who colored and grinned. "How'd you manage to hide them?" For I was worried about just that same thing. I couldn't turn these two away—we'd turned no one away yet, for all the strain it sometimes put on our resources. And I didn't want to tell this little boy he couldn't keep what were clearly his beloved pets. But how could we hide livestock? How could we make a quick getaway with dairy animals in tow?

"Watch this," Eric said. He climbed onto the branch of a nearby beech tree and whistled, and *the goats leapt up after him.* The bigger goat quickly conquered the next branch up, her full udder swinging—and she dislodged a very disgruntled Scarlet and Much, who had taken to sleeping away the daytime there.

Scarlet landed on my shoulder, still grumbling, but she faded quickly again into sleep. Much, who was a bit bolder, glared at the goats from midair, swooping in again and again to peck at them.

"Now, Much, don't be at that," Little Jane scolded, walking over to us. Anna Robin was nestled into a linen carrier Mae Tuck had fashioned, fast asleep on her mother's chest.

The old woman smiled at her. "What a lovely baby," she said. "How old is she?"

"Two months now," Little Jane replied. She kissed Anna Robin's fuzzy head.

"I'm glad to see a young mother here. Goat's milk is the best for babies, you know, after milk of your own. I bought Nanny here when Eric's mother died, and he thrived on it." She looked knowingly at Little Jane. "I imagine you might fancy getting a full night's sleep, and your little one will be no worse for a few drinks of fresh goat's milk. If you're willing, of course."

"Willing?" Little Jane laughed. "I'm likely to fall asleep while I stand. Would you really—You don't need all the milk yourself?"

The old woman shook her head, watching the roving, laughing groups in our clearing. Nell and Nellie Mason, who had proven to be surprisingly adept pickpockets, had just returned from Esting City and were showing off the fine jewelry and coins they'd nabbed to Kent, who praised them with admiring bemusement.

"I heard tell you share everything here," she said, "with them who need it. It's why we came. We need help"—her eyes looked briefly haunted, and I wondered what John had done to, or taken from, this sweet small family—"and I'll be only too glad if we can give it, too."

Little Jane was already lifting Anna Robin off her chest. "You're more welcome here than I can tell you," she said. She handed the baby to me, then gave her another kiss and one long look of infinite, wordless love. She looked up at the woman gratefully, the shadows under her eyes etched deep, and she walked off to take a long and deserved sleep.

Anna Robin buried her face against my neck.

"Babies know how to nurse," Eric informed me from the tree. "But I'll have to teach *you* how to milk."

❧ ❧

A few days later, Mae Tuck approached me as I finished milking Nanny, who had proved a generous contributor to our group.

"Silvie," she said, offering me a cup of tea, "are you and Bird lovers?"

I jerked, and a little milk spilled from my bucket. "No!"

The Mae smiled. "A good thing I hadn't handed this to you yet. Here, take it, but be ready for another shock. I want to talk frankly with you." She pressed the cup into my hands. Sitting down next to me, she continued: "I didn't think you were, but I see the way you look at him." She raised her eyebrows at me suggestively, then laughed.

I gave her a chagrined smile. "Probably everyone in the forest sees that, Mae Tuck. But just because . . ." Why was it so much harder to explain the way I felt out loud? "Bird and I have been great friends for so long, and now — He's the closest thing to family I have, out here. I gave up the rest of my family when I left Loughsley." That was harder to say that than I'd thought it would be, too. I found my throat catching. How could I be homesick for a prison? "If Bird and I were to — if we risked a romance, and then it failed, I would lose him. I couldn't bear that."

Mae Tuck looked at me searchingly. "You underestimate him, dear. And yourself. I've seen many couples in my time who have parted but remained friends."

"It's not just that," I said, although her words chipped away at some stubborn, brittle old defense I'd built up in myself. "I'm . . . free, out here. I'm bound to no one and nothing; none of us are."

"Love needn't be binding," she said. "Even a brief tryst can be a great blessing." She laughed again, gently. "I don't mean to push you any which way, Silvie, not at all. I only wanted to let you know I can help you, if you ever need it. Part of being a midwife is helping women keep unwanted babies from coming. There are poultices, herbs . . ." She dug into a pocket and pulled out a small bottle of clear liquid. "If you drink this before you sleep with a man," she said, "he won't get you with child, almost certainly. And if he does, there are other doses that can bring on your cycle, send the babe back to the Lady's care until you're ready. No one should be forced into motherhood." She looked fierce.

"She's right, Silvie," came a quiet voice behind us. Little Jane sat down on my other side, Anna Robin cradled in her arms. "It's hard enough to look after a baby you wanted to come."

I started. I realized I'd been assuming something about Little Jane, something crucial.

She glanced at me, then looked back down at Anna; she could never tear her gaze from her baby for long. "I went to Mae Tuck as soon as I missed my flux," she said. "I knew well what had happened to me, what was coming. I had plenty of time to decide what I wanted to do. We talked it over, all of it. She told me all the ways that she could help. Back then I thought . . . well, I told you what I thought. That I could keep my baby a secret until she came, and that by then my family would have to love her." She closed her eyes briefly. "I was wrong, and being so wrong about everyone I loved made me forget myself, forget that I wanted even my own life to go on, for a while. But even so . . . I always wanted her. Always."

Mae Tuck reached across me to press her hand to Little Jane's knee.

"Oh, Little Jane." I was in awe of her. I didn't know what to say.

"Take the medicine, anyway, Silvie," she urged. "You never know when you might need it." She winced. "I didn't mean — what happened to me. I only meant there might be a time when you want to use it."

We could hear Bird and Will Stutely trading jokes nearby. Seraph watched us from her perch on one of the tree house platforms. Both Little Jane and Mae Tuck were looking at me significantly.

"I understand!" I cried. "If I surrender to my so-obvious lusts I'll be sure to take caution!"

I hadn't intended to speak quite so loudly. The two women looked startled, and then all at once, together, we began to laugh.

❧ ❧

Little Jane, Bird, and I took our raptors out hunting together whenever we could, on the rare days that none of us had a more pressing duty to our growing forest family. Each of the birds was capable of bringing home kills on its own, but it was still good for Scarlet and Much to learn from Seraph's example, and Bird said following a peregrine's lead was one of the best ways to train them.

So we found ourselves, one evening at the dusky hour when the owlets had woken and the falcon had not yet gone to roost, in a part of the forest where we'd never been before. There was a fast-running stretch of river here, and Bird was sure that at this time of year, we would find salmon swimming upstream to spawn: perfect practice catches for Scarlet and Much. We watched through the delicate filigree of spring leaves as the three birds circled in the sky, waiting to spot their prey.

I heard a rustle and looked earthwards again. There, ahead of us, lumbering out of the gloom, so solid and massive that it could have been a great, living stone: a bear.

I felt myself change from hunter to prey in an instant. My heartbeat sped like a frightened rabbit's in my chest. I didn't let myself move; I knew well that the bear would chase us if we tried to run.

"Stay still," I whispered, trying to keep even my lips from moving too much. Bird was a hunter too, and he'd know; and surely Little Jane, growing up in a village so close to the forest, understood about bears, too.

But Anna Robin, only half-sleeping, grizzled in the wrap that kept her close to her mother's chest.

I ached. I pleaded. I was ready to pray to the Lord or the Lady or anyone else who might listen. *Not the baby.*

The bear rose onto its huge hind legs, sniffing the air. It looked at us. It looked at the river.

The bear called softly, lowering itself to earth again. Two smaller bulky shadows joined it, and the three made their way to the riverbank.

The larger bear cub tumbled into the water, splashing playfully. The other regarded the river with caution, but the mother nudged her small cub forward with her black velvet nose. Soon all three were cavorting in the stream. The mother made a sudden dive and came up with a glistening fish between her teeth; but she laid it on the riverbank carefully, and with infinite gentleness she nudged her children over to take part in the first catch.

"Come on," Little Jane said, backing smoothly away. "She'll let us go." She kissed Anna Robin's forehead. The baby gave a cry in earnest, and the mother bear's head rose sharply; I felt close to panic again, but she only watched us from the river, and turned back to her cubs as we four humans retreated.

❧ ❧

When we returned home, a new member of our forest family had arrived: a shy, small woman named Fay Carpenter.

Little Jane's mother.

She held Mae Tuck's arm as she walked towards us. She was trembling, and so pale I thought she was likely to faint. When she looked up into Little Jane's impassive face, and then at the bundle of Anna Robin on her chest, she began to weep.

"Jane I, I . . . I'm so sorry," she managed to say. "I . . . your father . . ."

"He lied," Little Jane said, her voice cool.

"I know, I . . ." Fay's eyes fluttered closed, and Mae Tuck pressed her arm. "I've left him, Jane. I've come here to . . . to find you, to help you, if you'll let me. Though I'll— understand if you don't want me here. It's so hard to become a mother when you don't have a . . . a mother yourself." Her eyes watered. "As soon as the Mae, here, told me what had happened to you, I wanted to come to you. But I didn't know where you'd gone; no one did. I never really believed your father about what you'd done, not in my heart. But even if it were true . . ." She shuddered. "I should have let nothing stop me from finding you. I'm your mother, Jane. I'm your mother. How I've failed you."

Little Jane closed her eyes, and I saw a few teardrops escape them. I put my arm around my friend as she crossed hers over her chest, cradling her own, now-sleeping baby.

I wanted to despise the woman in front of us, and for my friend's sake I would turn her away if I had to. But I would wait for Little Jane's word, for her decision.

"You told her what happened?" Little Jane spoke to Mae Tuck, not to her mother.

"Not just her," Mae Tuck said. "Why do you think John locked me up?" She looked at Little Jane compassionately, sadly. "I would never have broken our confidence, my child, if you had not vanished from the village," she continued, "but once you were gone, I felt I had to tell the truth about our young lord, our new sheriff. To be truthful I — I wanted to shame him. And shame your father, for disbelieving you."

"It's all right." Little Jane brushed off the tears that had scattered over her cheeks. "I'm . . . Mother, you really believe me?" Her voice was quiet, soft; a child's voice.

Fay nodded. She pulled away from Mae Tuck's support and began to reach out for her daughter, but hesitated. "I believe you, love," she said.

Little Jane began to smile. "Then I'm glad you're here," she said, and she gathered up her small mother in her great arms, the sleeping Anna Robin pressed between them.

# ~FOURTEEN~

# *Dancing in the May*

The rogues had been trying to persuade me out to a spring festival in Esting City, to see the Marian and dance the coming of the May. They were going to dress as women, Will Stutely told me.

"Is that part of the festival?" I asked—I'd never been to one before.

Arthur Tailor laughed. "Hardly," he said. "But we'll need some kind of disguise to avoid your brother's gaze, or that of any who would take his rewards."

Stutely grunted, already rummaging through one of the stacks of clothes that we kept for any who needed them. "Disguises are grand, but mostly I just fancied myself in that red petticoat, the night Little Jane's babe was born."

"*Everyone* fancied you in that petticoat," I said with a grin. "Red's your color, Stutely."

But he settled on a long, simple black dress and a veil drawn across his mouth and nose, in the manner of Su noblewomen, to hide his beard. He wore the disguise surprisingly well, moving elegantly, his eyes strikingly bright above the veil. In fact, many of the rogues made quite attractive women, it turned out.

I enjoyed watching them, but still I wanted to stay home with Little Jane and the baby.

Even that excuse, however, failed me.

"I've been wanting to get out of the forest again," Little Jane said, stroking Anna Robin's cheek as the baby nursed, but looking up at me with an expression that was more than a little haggard. "I've been feeling a little . . ."

"Cloistered?" Mae Tuck suggested. "Every new mother does. You're well healed now, Little Jane, and that baby would be content in the middle of an earthquake, I'd imagine. There's no reason you shouldn't go if you want to, and plenty of reason you should. It's always good to feel part of the world again." She smiled. "Besides, I'd like a chance to dance in the coming of the May myself, and to kiss the Marian."

I grinned at her slyly. "I thought the Brethren didn't approve of May festivals. My governesses always told me that we shouldn't celebrate the change of the seasons, only the grace of the Lord."

"The Brethren don't approve," Mae Tuck said, drawing herself up, "for the same reason they don't approve of my kind anymore. Too much earth and honesty and lusty abandon in a May festival. Too much human grace, which they don't think divine." She narrowed her gleaming eyes at me. "Always drawing sermons out of me, you are, Silvie."

I shrugged. "Can I help it if I like to learn?"

But it seemed there would be no way out of going to the May Festival after all.

⋙ ⋘

I had forgotten there were so many colors in the world. Streamers and ribbons of every hue decorated the streets of Esting City and the stalls that crowded them. Flowers, too: white, pink, yellow, red, purple—so many that the city air was almost as thick with glorious fresh smells as the forest had been. Not only the city wore flowers and ribbons; the people did, too, from infants to ancients.

In the center of the city was the main square. I'd thought it would be more crowded than anywhere else, but it was completely clear, the people staying off to the side streets. At its center a tall, intricately carved Maypole stretched thirty feet into the air, multitudes of ribbons tied around its top and fluttering in the breeze.

I took a big bite of the kidney pie I'd bought at a nearby stall, on Little Jane's recommendation. Its filling was tender and savory, with a gravy so delicious that I could hardly bear to swallow each bite.

Beside me Little Jane munched happily on an identical

pie. Like Mae Tuck and myself, she had disguised herself as a man for the festival; but she was less convincingly male than either of us, in spite of her size. The lines of her big body were emphatically feminine. Anna Robin was tucked securely in her wrap under the shirt Little Jane had borrowed from Stutely; her bulk could have been simply the belly of a man who ate and drank too much, to a stranger, but to me she simply radiated motherhood.

Still, at least the baby was quiet. "I think Mae Tuck was right," I told Little Jane through a mouthful. "That baby would sleep through anything."

"I'm lucky with her, that's for certain," she said, worship in her voice.

I looked toward the Maypole and saw a troubadour standing by it with a lute, a slim woman with long black hair and a spray of pink flowers tucked behind each ear. She bowed elaborately for the crowd, and one or two blossoms drifted to the ground.

I'd never seen Alana Dale before, but I knew her immediately: the most celebrated lady troubadour in Esting, but known even more for her legendary romantic adventures — with both men and women. A few weeks ago, Will Stutely had told a fireside story of the time a lady she loved had been imprisoned in a cloister by her disapproving parents. Alana had taken Sistren vows just to get into the convent and wrest her sweetheart from captivity. It was a delightful story, and Mae Tuck had laughed and sighed over it more than any of us.

Alana Dale was excommunicated after that, of course, but that had only increased her fame. She seemed right at home at the center of the May festivities.

"Make way for the Marian!" she cried, her strong voice carrying over the square, and quite possibly through the whole city.

The people around me began to back away toward the sides of the street. I moved with them, unsure of myself, but I found Little Jane and stood in front of her, protecting Anna Robin from being pressed too closely should the crowd grow too dense.

There was a path cleared now, along our street and toward the square. It was so crowded that I did not see the Marian until she was almost right in front of me.

A beautiful, wise-eyed young woman, clear of mind and clear of heart, Mae Tuck had said: the Marian was an embodiment of May itself.

I had imagined someone small and lithe, not unlike Alana. But the girl who walked before me with her crown of flowers had a plump and sturdy frame, as stocky as Little Jane, though not nearly so tall. She stood with her head held high and her shoulders back, and she smiled, it seemed, at every person in the crowd. In the moment when her eyes met mine, I saw indeed what Mae Tuck had meant about their being wise, and I knew that whoever had selected the Marian had chosen well. I saw depth and kindness in her gaze, a kind of beauty that could never be pretended, or even imitated.

She was beautiful in other ways, too: red hair streamed down her back in waves, her creamy skin was starred with amber freckles, and those wise eyes were the clear color of melting river water. Every plump limb and generous curve was perfect. Her white dress and crown of flowers made her seem indeed the embodiment of springtime.

She broke eye contact with me almost instantly, but it was impossible not to keep watching her as she walked into the center of the square.

She picked up the flowers the troubadour had lost and offered them back to her, making a simple curtsey. Alana Dale took the blossoms and tucked them in her hair, kissed the Marian's hand, and performed her low bow again, losing three more flowers in the process.

The crowd laughed, not unkindly.

The Marian picked up the three flowers, and after a brief smiling, questioning glance to the troubadour, tossed them into the crowd.

I didn't see who caught them, for Alana began to play her lute, and the Marian to dance.

She chose a pink ribbon from the mass that were tied

at the top of the pole, held it overhead, and began to sway back and forth in time to the music. She lifted one foot and then the other; it was only then that I noticed she wasn't wearing shoes.

The Marian swept around the square, lifting her ribbon high, until she had wrapped it three times around the pole. The music had grown faster, jubilant, and I found it hard not to move my own feet. The Marian made a beckoning motion with one hand, and several people stepped forward. Each of them took up a ribbon and they joined her in delicate, leaping circles, in a dance they all clearly knew.

"Are you all right?" I looked back at Little Jane, still worried that someone would push against her or Anna.

She smiled. "I'm fine. I think someone wants to dance with you."

"Thanks, Little Jane," a voice behind me said, "but I can ask her myself."

I turned and Bird was there, one hand outstretched. The cotton dress and kerchief he was wearing disguised him, but there was no mistaking the broad hand he held out to me, or the hazel eyes I knew so well; the green he wore brought out their color. "Well, Silvie?" he asked, giving a wry, half-joking curtsey. "Will you dance in the May with me?"

I returned his curtsey with a gallant bow, and we laughed. But there was no point ignoring the fast beating of my heart when I nodded and put my hand in his, or the way I couldn't quite catch my breath when we ran lightly toward the square together. Although I'd danced plenty of times before, even with Bird, when we were young, I'd never danced in the May, nor weaved my way through such a crowd before. But I knew well that wasn't why my pulse had sped up.

There was no point ignoring it, but I didn't have to dwell on it, either. So we took our portion of the joy that flowed through every dancer in the square; I could feel it like a spark in my fingers when I took up the end of a red ribbon. Next to me Bird caught up a pale green one.

I knew what to do from the moments I'd spent watching; the dance was a simple one, and it had always come easy to me, dancing. Bird and I rushed off in opposite directions, weaving our ribbons over and under the others. We made wide circles that nearly reached the buildings at the edge of the square on our first round, and it was two or three minutes before I caught even a glimpse of my so-called partner again. When I did, it was only to touch hands with him briefly as we crossed paths, the way I did with every dancer who moved widdershins, opposite me.

But each time we circled each other the ribbons shortened, weaving together in a tight plaited pattern around the pole, so that the two circles of dancers were drawn inexorably closer and closer together, having to duck increasingly low or even leap right over each other. At last the pole was covered in tightly woven ribbons almost down to the height of our heads, and the dancers' arms stretched out to keep hold of their ends.

With a last burst of music, every hand that held a ribbon touched the pole almost at once, and the dancers found themselves on top of each other, torsos and arms and legs tangled together.

And I was face to face with Bird.

The chaos of overlapping ribbons had been perfectly arranged all along; we each were reunited with the partner with whom we had entered the dance.

Bird was warm against me, always so warm, and the spring day was cool even in this frolicking crowd.

I was the man now; the dance was mine to lead. I touched Bird's waist and he put his hand on my shoulder; we clasped our other hands and were off.

He was a good dancer, too, and our feet followed each other with ease. I had to keep one eye on the couples around us, to make sure we followed their pattern. It helped me keep from looking too long into Bird's eyes. Through the fall and winter, I had pretended that the heat between us was only what we needed to keep warm. It wasn't so easy to pretend now, in the pulse of spring, dancing in the May with a hundred other smiling couples.

No. Easier to watch those others, and smile, and know

that my time for that kind of warmth hadn't yet come, that I still wanted freedom more than warmth.

Steeling my heart with that new determination, I was able to look into his face at last—and I found that he was angry. His eyes were hard, and in the next moment he dropped my hand and began to walk away through the weave of the other dancers.

Only half a beat later the music ended, and all the couples parted. I didn't think anyone else could have noticed. Yet I felt as suddenly cold as if someone had ripped a cloak from my shoulders, a blanket from my bed while I slept.

Still, if he wanted to go, I couldn't ask him to stay. That had always been important to me. I found the side of the square where I'd stood with Little Jane and Mae Tuck and walked back toward them, trying to feel the sun on my skin and smell the flowers in the air, trying to pretend I didn't feel so cold.

Little Jane wasn't there.

I lectured myself not to worry, reminded myself of all the times I'd witnessed her remarkable strength and resilience in the past months, but all my protective instincts toward her leapt up in my heart in spite of myself. I looked around, my pulse rising, my wide-brimmed hat whipping against my cheeks as I turned—it would be hard to miss someone as tall as Little Jane, even in this big a crowd . . .

And yet I saw Will Stutely first, the vivid blue of his eyes over his veil, his powerful shoulders—and his arm around Little Jane, and hers around him. They were laughing together as they walked away from the dancing, in exactly the manner of friends, yet the admiration in Stutely's eyes as he looked at Little Jane was not simply that of friendship.

It was something I'd seen in him, I realized, since his first morning in the forest, but I hadn't put a name to it.

"So what happens next?" I asked as they joined me.

"The king is coming in," said Stutely. "He'll bless the Marian."

I raised my eyebrows. "The *king* comes to this?"

"Of course. The prince would be here, too, if he weren't away on that inane mission of his."

My father had told me that none of the nobility participated in these ancient seasonal festivals. I thought of how sure I'd been, over the course of the autumn and winter, that part of the problem with this country was how disconnected the nobles had become from such things. But I'd known, too, that my genteel, urbane father had a personal dislike for anything remotely connected to the dirt and cold and wet and . . . asymmetry of the natural world.

He'd lied to me, and that was the fact of it. The king came to bless the Marian, and if the prince were here he would have danced in the May with the rest of us. I could hardly believe it.

Trumpets sounded, a much more formal and regal

sound than the joyous rough strings and singing that had accompanied the dancing. A procession of nobles walked up onto the covered platform at one end of the square and took their seats along a row of plushly cushioned chairs. They were smiling, laughing, brightly clothed, and I recognized more than a few of them. There was Clara, even, with her drugged little dog . . .

John wasn't among them, king's sheriff or no. I realized I'd been waiting to see him, dreading to see him, ever since we'd left the forest. My relief swept through me so strongly that I began to tremble.

I reached out for Bird at my side, simply by instinct. But he hadn't come back after the dance; he wasn't there. I didn't know where he was.

I stepped closer to Little Jane and Stutely but still felt cold.

The king came last of all, of course, and accompanied by the greatest fanfare yet.

He raised a hand, and the music stopped.

He began a rote speech about the greatness of Esting and its culture, but I ignored his words, scanning the crowd for Bird. He wasn't there, but still I didn't want to listen to the king, didn't want to hear the hypocrisy of his praise for a kingdom that starved its populace so that he and his nobles could wear riches like they wore that day, so that his spoiled son could decide no woman deserved him and launch himself off on a cripplingly expensive romantic adventure.

That is, I couldn't bear to listen until Clara began to speak. She stepped forward with several other court ladies whom I vaguely recognized. They wore fine, gauzy spring dresses, and each had a spray of almond blossoms pinned over her heart.

"Thank you for letting us speak, Your Majesty," Clara said. She and her friends curtsied in perfect unison. She turned to face the crowd. "We wear these flowers to show our sympathy with the poor and destitute of Esting. We have begun a Ladies' Fund in the royal court, and we are raising money to give to the Brethren's efforts to aid the less fortunate. Our women-in-waiting will be selling corsages like these today for five crowns, and the dresses that Lady Julia, Lady Constance, and I are wearing will be auctioned at the end of the festival." She and her friends turned to each side, showing off the beautiful, expensive clothes that, auction or no, they would never deign to wear a second time.

"Thank you for your attention." They curtsied again and retreated to stand behind the king once more.

"Five crowns!" I whispered.

Mae Tuck shook her head in amazement.

I found that I was nearly shaking with anger. I had no doubt of Clara's good intentions, but who exactly did she think was going to buy little bouquets of exotic imported flowers at such an exorbitant price? We'd left three crowns at each house in Woodshire Village after our caper with the Brethren carriage, knowing that the sum would see them through the winter. None of the commoners here could afford such a price, and few of the nobles would want to.

"You know just what the court's Brethren will do with that money, too," Mae Tuck murmured, "and it isn't feed the hungry, I can tell you that."

"And who do they think will bid on the dresses? No one in the crowd can afford them, and no noblewoman would be caught dead in a dress another lady has already worn . . ."

The Mae nodded. "The king let her speak because it makes him look charitable. The ladies get to show off their kind hearts, to believe they're doing good, without making any real change to the way things are. He'd never let them speak if they posed any serious threat." She raised her eyebrows and shot me a smile. "True change requires radical action—like ours in the forest. Like yours, Silvie. You made a real change, took real risks, to help your people. You're not just play-acting at charity."

I shook my head. My anger at Clara's naivety was starting to leave me, and in its place was a sickly kind of self-loathing. I'd abandoned my comfortable life at Loughsley, but I had never known, could never know, the hardships that most of the people in Esting faced.

Clara and her ladies were smiling at each other smugly behind the king, certain of their own goodness. Was I really so different from those preening, posing nobles?

I saw Princess Ghazia—the Su princess who'd been at the Hunt Ball, brought in to woo Rioch—watching Clara, and there was doubt clearly written in her eyes above her veil. I wondered what she and her attendants thought of this farce.

I froze with sudden shock. Someone else had moved forward to stand near the king. At his side, tall and fierce, surveying the crowd with barely restrained violence and contempt in his eyes, was the sheriff.

John.

# ~FIFTEEN~

# *Alana and Ghazia*

I stepped in front of Little Jane before I let myself think about anything else. Above all John must not see Little Jane with a baby, must not see Anna. That he mustn't see me, either, hardly mattered in comparison.

Behind me, I could feel Little Jane's energy drain away as she noticed my brother, too. Stutely was at my side at once, lending his broad frame to the shield I was trying to make.

"Crouch down a little, if you can," I muttered, not daring to turn around. "Once you're far enough away from the square, go to the forest. We'll join you there soon. Mae Tuck, go with her."

Little Jane and the Mae vanished, and the spaces they left in the crowd were filled at once. Finally I felt as if I could breathe.

But John wasn't even looking at the crowd anymore. After the applause for the king died down—how could they clap for a man who'd taken so much of their lifeblood?

—he conferred briefly with the monarch, then walked around the dais and toward the Maypole in the center of the square. Alana Dale didn't move, even when it became clear that she was blocking the path he wanted to take. He glared at her, stared her down with the malevolent gaze I'd seen him direct, over the course of my life, toward almost everyone but me; it had never proven ineffective.

Yet the troubadour held his gaze, smirking. She started down into the bow she'd given the Marian, then turned it into a mocking little pirouette. She took her lute and prodded its neck into John's chest, just as if it were a knife. "A tune for you, Sheriff?" she asked, sarcastically deferent.

Around me the whole crowd laughed: another story to tell of the lady troubadour, playing out before their eyes. But the last thing I felt able to do was to laugh with them.

"One for you, my dear," said John, in tones that were anything but endearing. "Here's a story for you, friends"—addressing the crowd—"this minstrel is the Forest Queen."

He seized the neck of Alana's lute and wrenched it from her with one hand. With the other, he grabbed the girl herself, then casually dropped the fine instrument; it fell to the cobblestones, and in the sudden silence of the crowd I could hear the ping of strings breaking.

"The Forest Queen?" I murmured blankly to Stutely.

He frowned down at me. "How can you not know . . . ?"

I remembered what one of the rogues had said, the night they had joined our band. "To follow the forest's queen . . ." I shivered.

"The criminal who has raided your coffers all winter," John said, nodding toward the dais, to the king and all the nobles, "has been laughing at you all this time. And you've been laughing with her! Applauding her! No more. Today the Forest Queen becomes queen of the dungeon—or of the noose." He turned, wrenching Alana so that she was forced to turn with him, and he nodded deferentially to the king. "As you decree, Your Majesty."

The king beckoned, and a black-robed priest approached from the shadows and leaned over his throne. The king murmured a question, or a series of questions, judging by how long he took to speak. Whatever the priest's reply, it was very short. A word or two and he receded into the shadows at the back of the dais again.

"Any traitor must take the noose," the king said.

John nodded. "Then we shall add a public hanging to the May festivities," he said.

I felt a kind of horror I'd never known when another cheer went up. Not a hearty one, and not from everyone in the crowd, but it was there.

Alana Dale kept that bold smile on her face, that charm. And as John began to lead her away, she started to sing.

*Slack your rope, hangman; slack it for a while.*
*I think I see my mother coming, riding many a*
*mile . . .*

It was the first few bars of an old folk ballad; I'd heard
several of the rogues singing it in the forest over the winter,
and even Bird would whistle it once in a while.

Alana's voice broke, but she laughed as it failed her.

The Forest Queen. I knew that John, in his way, was
protecting me by claiming that the title belonged to someone else. That he would protect me by killing this charming
songbird, and that it would be nothing to him to do so.

"Stutely," I said, "how long will it take to gather the
rogues?"

He chuckled, low and harsh. Then he gave a whistle
that pierced the air, and I saw a dozen pairs of eyes, two
dozen, more, turn toward us, and more than two dozen
bodies begin to move through the crowd. "Done," he said.
"We're ready at your word, my queen." There was none of
the teasing I wanted to hear in his voice when he gave me
that title.

I didn't have time to worry about why I was the one
leading them, or why they were following my orders. I
knew what the Forest Queen had to do.

"Keep them spread around the square. We'll take her as
soon as we can; you'll know the moment."

Stutely nodded, and I stepped forward, out of the crowd. I prayed Little Jane and Mae Tuck were well clear of this place by now.

"Let Alana go," I said. "She's innocent. She's not the Forest Queen." I threw my hat to the ground with what I hoped was a suitably dramatic gesture. I needed this story to spread, too, or John would just choose another victim. I needed everyone in Esting City to see that *I* was the Forest Queen.

John had stopped walking, but he hadn't turned back to look at me. I could see the angry movement of his shoulders as he breathed. I could see the firm grip he had on Alana Dale's arms as he wrenched them up against her back.

Slowly he turned around. When I finally saw his face, it was indescribably sad. "You were gone, Silvie," he whispered. "You would have been safe after this. You could have come back . . ." The sadness in his face was draining away. Rage was taking its place, frosty and hard. "A fool at every turn. So stubborn. When I only wanted—"

What my brother wanted was just what I had always been running from.

"Now!" I told Stutely.

He tackled John, and the band of rogues rushed forward. For a moment it looked as though all the women in the square were closing in on the sheriff. It was a beautiful thing to witness, but I couldn't watch. I only had time to wrench Alana Dale's arms from his grasp and tell her to run.

❧ ❧

I tugged her along as we pushed through the crowd. I'd come to be able to run very fast in the forest, and I could hardly expect a city-dwelling troubadour to keep up, but I sensed it was something else that kept her following more slowly, almost clumsily.

I couldn't ask her, couldn't even stop to look at her. "Do you want to hang?" I asked, still running as the city gave way to village houses, and then to a country highway, and at last the graceful, shifting green world of Woodshire Forest wrapped its arms around the two of us.

I didn't stop running until we were well within the treeline, and even then, I only looked for a sufficiently low-branched tree before hoisting myself up and then reaching down to help Alana after me. I was sure I could hear footsteps — soldiers' footsteps, John's . . .

*Don't think about it. Just think about getting away.*

We were up in a white pine, high enough that we couldn't be seen even if they were still following us, even if they could somehow read our footsteps on a cobblestone road, could tell just where we'd left the road for the forest.

*They can't,* I told myself over and over. *He can't.*

I finally let myself rest and look at Alana. She was

doubled over on the branch next to me, panting, I thought in pain . . . but no.

She was laughing.

I began to feel sick with dread.

"Did you—Oh, Lady and Lord," I said. "You were part of it, weren't you? He wanted me to rescue you, to lead him back here—" I started to shake, so hard I was in danger of falling out of the tree.

Alana's laughter stopped abruptly.

She narrowed her eyes at me: they were an unremarkable shade of light brown, but just as intense in their expression as I remembered Stutely describing in his story. "Who, the sheriff? Not at all. Wouldn't do that bully's bidding for a kingdom—or please him to avoid a noose, as you saw yourself. It's just . . ." She laughed again. "I've never been the *damsel in distress* in one of my own adventures before. I quite enjoyed it, with such a lovely rescuer!"

I found myself smiling at her.

"And I've been meaning to do a song about the Forest Queen. You've given me a great gift, my dear." She winked at me, and heat rose in my cheeks. Chagrined, I turned away and waved for her to follow me. It was only about two hours' walk through the canopy until we'd reach the haven again, although it would likely take longer with a companion unused to walking on branches—even if the light-footed Alana already seemed surprisingly adept.

"What gift was that?" I asked.

She began to whistle a tune I recognized as a jauntier version of "The Maid Freed from the Gallows," which she'd sung in the square.

"Why, inspiration," she said, laughing again.

⁓ ⁓

Our supper in the forest that night was the most raucous yet. Stutely and Arthur cavorted in front of the fire, reenacting the "distraction" they'd provided at the festival.

"Woe is me: a maiden at the May festival without a lover!" Stutely pitched his voice high and clasped his hands over his heart.

Arthur leapt up next to him. "And I! But perhaps we can comfort each other?"

They moved in for an embrace, and Arthur swooned back in Stutely's arms. "What big, strong hands you have, dear lady," he said.

"All the better to—" Stutely hefted Arthur upright and spun around, swinging a fist through the air. "And—there! The first guard never knew what hit him."

"None of them did," Arthur said. "And except for the sheriff and a few of his men, most of them were right hesitant to fight back against women, too. It was easy as walking to flatten the lot of them."

Alana grinned. "Now that deserves a song, my lads! I'll

have to see what I can do." She toasted them and took a long drink. We'd opened more of Mae Tuck's bramble wine, to celebrate both the May and our victory, and the rogues were carousing—and well deserving of it, too.

Little Jane sat close by the fire, nursing Anna Robin, Mae Tuck at her side. Part of me wanted to join them, but I found myself keeping apart from the group, scanning the trees for a certain figure, or the patches of night sky for the dark blot of a falcon's wings. But Bird still hadn't come back. I hadn't seen him since our dance.

Scarlet stayed close to me, even though most nights lately she'd been following Much on hunting expeditions, fruitlessly trying to learn to catch her own dinner. She kept pecking at the hem of my cloak, fidgeting with my sleeves, but she wouldn't take any of the bits of food I offered her.

Bird wasn't around to admonish me for feeding Scarlet as if she were still an owlet, for not letting her get hungry enough to *need* to learn to hunt effectively. I took a little extra-frustrated pleasure in trying to feed my owl, knowing that the vanished Bird would disapprove.

She wasn't eating, but she wouldn't stop worrying my hems, glaring at me with those huge yellow eyes.

I heard a frustrated hoot near the fire and looked up to see Much fluttering around Little Jane's head. He wouldn't go close enough to risk scratching or pecking the baby, but he was trying to kick up what fuss he could. Little Jane flicked him away halfheartedly, her eyes nearly closing in exhaustion. Even with the milk from Eric's goats, of which there was enough for his grandmother to make cheese with as well as to feed Anna at night, and even with all of our band's help, motherhood was exhausting for her.

I stood up to go offer to hold the baby for a while.

As soon as I stood, Scarlet let out a shriek and flew for the edge of the clearing. When I didn't follow, she circled back to me and landed on my shoulder, digging in her talons more fiercely than she'd ever done. She and Much were both staring out at the forest.

I froze, suddenly understanding.

There was someone there.

"All right, Scarlet," I whispered, forcing myself not to look too quickly or obviously where my owl was leading me. I caught Stutely's eye and tilted my head ever so slightly, and he gave an infinitesimal nod. After a few moments, he drained his tin mug and stood, moving casually in the direction of the wine casks—and toward the place my owl was directing us.

I was grateful that my cloak hid the motion as I reached for my dagger. I reached up with my other hand and stroked Scarlet, murmuring to her in what I hoped seemed a nonchalant way.

My eyes had adjusted to the firelight; even though I'd

learned to be good at seeing the shapes of living things in the trees in my years on the hunts, I struggled to find what my owl so clearly saw. Was it there — a dark shape, crouched on a branch as lightly and easily as a bird, as my Bird?

I hardly had time to have the thought before the shape leapt from the trees and felled me. I saw a veiled face, and for a wild moment I thought it was Stutely, still in his disguise from the May festival — but then I saw the real Stutely over me, too, making a dive at my attacker that would surely fell anyone.

But it didn't. The veiled figure made a fluid motion so fast and graceful it reminded me of Much diving for a kill, and then Stutely was on the ground, too, laid out by my side as neatly as trussed game.

"Now," said our assailant, in a regal and lightly accented voice that seemed to fill the whole clearing. "Now that I have proven my worth in combat, I will take the place I have earned in your party."

A veiled woman with a Su accent, an expert fighter who spoke like a noble. I realized that I knew her, or at least I knew of her.

"Princess Ghazia," I said. The name came out of me in a wheeze.

She nodded. Stutely and I sat up, rubbing our chests.

"Honored to meet you," she said, dipping an Estinger-style curtsey. The gauzy layers of her black dress and veil fluttered.

"At least a dozen guards were posted around our group tonight," I said. *All of them sharp and well able to fight, and armed with the best of Loughsley's weapon stores,* I thought. "How did you get past them?"

Ghazia scoffed. "I stayed in the shadows, and I move fast."

"That you do," Stutely said, still rubbing his breastbone.

"And I can look like a shadow myself, in these." She touched her dark clothes, her veil, with her fingertips; even that motion had speed and grace to it. "You have no idea of the freedom the veil affords me. No Estinger does, thankfully, or I would not be here tonight." I saw by her eyes that she was beginning to smile. "It saved me from your boorish prince falling in love with my beautiful face, for instance," she said.

There was nervous laughter in several trees now, from the guards who should have stopped Ghazia from coming.

"I would have had to marry him for the good of my kingdom, and I've seen how the Esting elite treat their people," she said, growing serious. "Such abuses as you have suffered would never be tolerated in the Sudlands. Besides"—the smile came into her eyes again—"I've found that my tastes run elsewhere." She curtsied once more, this time toward Alana Dale, who was watching her with an expression I imagined was not unlike that of someone who has just been struck by lightning.

"Sadly, however," the princess went on, "I have come here not in the name of romance, but to offer my help."

"How do we know we can trust you?" The voice from behind me was that of Kent Mason. I turned to see him standing by the fire, his arm around his wife. Nellie was not at her usual place by her mother's side—in fact, I hadn't seen her since I'd returned from the city.

She seemed to have vanished about the same time Bird had.

I pushed that thought from my mind.

"You're one of them," Kent continued. "A noble. A *princess*." His voice dripped with scorn, but I was relieved and proud that it held not a trace of fear.

"And your leader is the Lady of Loughsley," Ghazia replied. "Besides, you all heard today what everyone in court is calling her."

Her use of my title was a jarring reminder. I hadn't thought of myself as a lady for so long, it sounded like a lie to hear it spoken now.

"The Forest Queen," said Alana Dale. "And ooh, how it rankles the king, and the sheriff, too."

"How he goes on about it!" Ghazia took the opportunity

to move closer to Alana, and the minstrel made room for the princess to sit with her by the fire.

"'The forest is chaotic,' the sheriff says," Ghazia went on. "'It has no order, no discipline, no court, no law.' He sees the world like a chessboard, I think, your sheriff does—and a forest has no straight lines. That someone else might have figured out how to rule such a place, someone who isn't him . . .'"

*He sees the world like a chessboard.* I stared at Ghazia, stunned: she had seen so little of him, but she was precisely right. She'd articulated something about him that I'd never been able to: John's casual, merciless cruelty to anyone he thought had less power than he, and his fawning charm with those in higher positions. His life, his world, was a game and a battle, exactly like chess. He'd made himself into a powerful player for his king, and our group in the forest was his opposing side.

And I his opposing queen . . .

"He's planned his next move," Ghazia said. "That is what I came to tell you. He hates the stories that are being told about you, the way those stories are inciting rebellion. He has the king convinced that you're not just thieves, but revolutionaries. He thinks you're planning a war, and they've increased their taxes yet again so that Esting's army can fight back. They're going to stamp you out."

"Revolutionaries?" I looked around at our merry camp,

at Little Jane and Anna Robin by the fire, at the Masons, at
Will Stutely and the rogues, at the many families and in-
dividuals who had come here because — because John had
forced them to come, because they had nowhere else to go.
"We're not soldiers," I said. "We're just trying to keep everyone alive, and fed, and free."

Ghazia laughed. "What is that if not rebellion, when
those who rule you want you hungry and indentured?"
She shook her head. "What a strange place this is. Tyrants
who call themselves noble, and rebels who claim they aren't
fighting at all."

"She's right, Silvie," Little Jane said. Anna Robin had
fallen asleep at her breast. She adjusted her dress to cover
herself and handed her baby to Mae Tuck, who stroked the
infant's cheek adoringly. When Little Jane looked at me, her
expression was fearsome. "If someone wants to take from
you, break you, make you wish you were dead, as the sheriff
and the king have done, as John did to me . . . if someone doesn't care whether you live or die, then living itself is
rebellion."

I could still feel the rope in my hands with Little Jane's
weight at the end of it. I knew she'd earned her convictions,
earned every one of the words she spoke.

"We are rebels, Silvie, if only because we're living our
own lives, not the ones they'd choose for us. Not the ones
your brother would choose. And living is . . . Just living *is*

fighting, sometimes. Living on after the night I met you has taught me that. So has having Anna."

I nodded. The group around the fire took on a different cast: strong bodies, strong hearts, each of us in our different way contributing to a life that was better for all of us than the lot our unjust kingdom had cast us. We were rebelling, not just when we stole and redistributed the nobles' and the Brethren's money, but every time we laughed together, ate together, built shelter for each other, or dressed each other's wounds. Every night Bird kept a fire burning in the forest.

It was my turn to keep that fire burning now.

"We have to move before John does," I said, standing. "If we're at war, then we're going to win."

❧ ❧

"Silvie?" Lady Clara Halving stared at me from her bed, clutching silk sheets to her chest. "Silvie, what are you doing here?"

I smiled at her. "Did you mean it when you said you wanted to help Esting's poor?"

# ~SIXTEEN~

# Steal from the Rich, Give to the Poor

Clara's taste for palace guards had endured since the Hunt Ball, but I'd hardly dared to hope that their regard for *her* would be so strong. Drawing two of them away from their posts by the treasury door was the work of a moment—or of a low-cut nightdress and a sultry look.

"If this is what you mean by justice, darling, count me in," she'd murmured to me before sidling up to the guards. I smiled, keeping myself well hidden behind one of the long hall's marble pillars.

"I've some friends in my chambers tonight. We've been amusing ourselves, but we wanted a little male company . . . That David Doncaster wouldn't be here tonight, would he? Not that he *quite* holds a candle to you, James . . ."

Watching her lead them away, I found it hard not to laugh. There were friends waiting in Clara's room, all right:

a dozen rogues in the same women's clothes they'd worn to the May Festival.

Perched on my shoulder, Scarlet watched, too. Bird was right that she wasn't much of a hunter, but she was a loyal companion — and a silent one, when she needed to be.

All the time we had spent planning this heist, all through the night Ghazia had appeared and the following two days, I had been waiting for Bird to return. We had worked in shifts through the nights, building and building under Little Jane's directions, and I had hardly slept myself. I couldn't focus on him, not when there were so many more important things to plan and think about, but the wondering and the hurt were there, a hollow space in my chest — especially since Nellie hadn't come back, either.

Still, I was glad he wasn't here now, I told myself. This was a plan I had created, without his help or advice or his condescension, his insistence on my naivety and his own clearsighted, practical wisdom.

It would have been easy to let anger at his sudden abandonment overwhelm me, as easy as it would have been to succumb to missing him while all of us in the forest made our plan.

But if we succeeded, I would have time to feel as many things as I liked. And Bird would know, and John, and everyone, exactly what kind of person I was.

I slipped out of the shadows and into the royal treasury.

I unlooped the thin rope hanging at my side and held one end up to Scarlet's beak. She grasped it and swooped silently toward the vent in the treasury's ceiling, and I took up the first bag of gold coins.

⚬◦⚬ ◦⚬

The rogues' shadows lined the palace rooftop like turrets. Below us, more than fifty other members of our forest family waited, ready to receive our spoils and pass them on.

The North River cuts through the middle of Esting City, separating the palace from the citizenry like a moat. The same river that weaves through Woodshire Forest, that flows in front of Loughsley Abbey and under the Wedding-Ring Bridge. The same river on whose banks so many of Esting's villages are founded, the river that connects our whole country indiscriminately.

The river that, this night, would feed us all.

The spoils I'd found in the treasury had sickened me: the riches of centuries of noble greed had accrued there, jewels and precious metal and coin. Left in a dark room, doing no one any good. I'd worked quickly, pocketing as many treasures as I could and tying much more to the rope Scarlet had fed up to the roof, where the rogues were waiting.

The finery sparkled even in the nighttime darkness as we handed it down and down and down to the river's edge. Mae Tuck and Nell Mason, waiting by the water, formed the last link in the chain we made down from the palace rooftop. I could see the cold shine of the first piece of metal when it reached them, and they loaded it into the first of the boats we had made.

There were hundreds of them, the smallest barely the size of two cupped hands, the largest not quite big enough to bear a person down the river—but big enough to hold riches from the treasury; a sack of grain from the palace kitchen's vast pantries; several bolts of warm, thick cloth; or a small collection of weapons from the armory. All of us together, even with the experienced thieves and the lock-smiths and everyone else who had brought their own particular talents to this one great effort, had not managed to clear the palace stores of their excess wealth.

But we had come fairly close. We had taken enough to feed and clothe the people of a hundred small Esting villages—and arm them, too. Every little boat set upon the river started off in its own direction, pulled wherever the current sent it.

The idea had been mine, the design for the boats a collaboration between Little Jane, Arthur, and Stutely. Every person in the forest family who had able hands had helped to build them. It was hard not to shake from weariness, but watching all the collected wealth of the palace flow out to the people who needed it sent a rush of relief and pride and energy through my body.

I thought of Little Jane, exhausted and loving, nursing her baby. It was time for our country to feed its people.

❦ ❦

Little Jane was waiting for me back in the forest, and she flung her arms open as I jumped down from the trees and ran to her. We made room for Anna Robin, who was sleeping in her wrap, between us as we embraced.

"It went well, then?" she asked eagerly, pulling back to look at me. "Your smile says it did. Oh, I would love to have seen it—tell me everything."

But I didn't need to. I simply took her hand and led her down to the stream.

This one small offshoot of the North River was not yet crowded with bounty; as we approached it, the stream was quiet and empty under the moonlight. But in only a few minutes, one of the little boats we had made floated into view. It was one of the smaller ones, the size of a large platter. A satchel of copper coins weighing perhaps a stone was strapped to it.

I waited for the parcel to reach our part of the stream, and then I waded out a few steps and caught it. I held it out to Little Jane, my hands dripping. "See?"

Her eyes glowed warmly in the darkness. "It worked perfectly."

I set the boat and the offering it carried back into the water, and it drifted calmly away from us.

"In the morning," I said, "people all over Esting will be waking up to food, clothing, money."

"Hope," Little Jane murmured, stroking Anna's hair. "Survival."

∞ ∞

When we got back to the clearing, Mae Tuck was setting up another bonfire. I was surprised to see a light glowing inside the cave, too.

"You kept Bird's fire going?" I asked the Mae.

"No . . ." she said. "It's only been the few of us here, and we've all stayed in the clearing, waiting for news. Safer together." She frowned. "That fire should have died down to coals by now."

I was already walking away from them and toward the cave. He was back, Bird was back, and I was so angry with him for leaving, so eager to see him again—

The cave was empty. I peered into the darkness beyond the bright circle of the fire, and I even walked the cave's perimeter, but no one was there. Bird wasn't there. Someone who had stayed in the forest, one of the dozen or so who had young children to mind or who weren't strong or quick enough to help in our palace raid, must have stoked it while I was gone.

Of course they had. Once Bird did something, he committed to it absolutely. It was foolish to think he'd come back.

But feeling that hope and then losing it so quickly had pulled away the happy rush I'd felt as I moved through the trees after our mighty success, as I had shown Little Jane the victory that was sweeping down the rivers all over the country. I felt the full weight of three days' sleepless exhaustion, and all I wanted to do was rest.

Outside, some of the quickest rogues were returning; even the fastest of them took at least half an hour longer to get back to our stronghold than I had, moving through the trees. They were getting ready for a midnight supper. It wouldn't be a celebratory feast, since all of us had spent our strength to the last; it would be a functional meal of nourishment and a few happy whispers before sleeping the sleep of the just.

But I found I wasn't even able to do that. I wanted, for just a little while, to be alone.

I went to sleep in the empty cave while the rest of our party still murmured together by the bonfire. I couldn't sleep in the tree houses with everyone else, not that night.

The hammocks still hung by the walls, but even with several blankets and my cloak, it took me a long time to get warm. I remembered my first nights in the cave with Bird with angry longing. He had his freedom as much as I did,

I reminded myself; no, more so. I couldn't make him stay always at my side, as if he were Scarlet; even birds had their freedom, and they hunted the better for it.

As if to remind me, Scarlet landed with a low hoot next to me. She had, shockingly, caught herself a mouse. She shook her head, the little creature dangling from her beak, displaying it to me with pride. Then she swallowed it in one gulp.

"Good girl, Scarlet," I said, half asleep at last. I heard the rustle of wings as she left me again.

I pictured Bird with real wings like an owl's, flying high above the canopy, dancing circles around the moon the way we'd woven our way around the Maypole. I kept thinking of those wings, that freedom, to lull myself to sleep, and I tried to use them to color my dreams.

But my old nightmare claimed me again. Tangled and bound in the bedroom of a nameless palace, a faceless bridegroom advancing on me . . .

I woke, startled, taking gasps of air that felt thin in my lungs and tasted somehow wrong. I pushed at my blankets, even though they were finally warm, just wanting my limbs to be free, to be free . . . Sleep made me so sluggish, and the air was so wrong . . .

I wasn't tied down, but there was someone standing over me. A tall, broad-shouldered figure, faceless in the darkness.

Not Bird.

My brother.

# ~SEVENTEEN~

## In Ruins

O h, Silvie," he said. "You let me find you at last. I knew you wanted me to."

It was just like the nightmare again. The air felt thin and acrid; my breath caught in my throat, my voice strangled to nothingness. John wasn't touching me, not even a hand on the blankets, but he was close enough, close enough to touch . . .

The knife. I kept my garter on even while I slept, and I'd finally grown used to it; sleeping on my side as I was, I thought I could reach down under my blanket before John would know just what I was doing.

But for another few painful seconds, I couldn't make myself move. My blankets and cloak felt too much like the bedclothes that had tied me down in those dreams, and the monster bridegroom was here, here at last, and I was overcome with the horrible, unknowable understanding that I'd always known exactly whose face I would see if I lit my lamp and held it out . . .

I forced myself out of the nightmare. I was waking, and I could move. I grasped for the knife at my side.

John's man was on me before my hand could reach it. He wrenched the blankets around me, binding me fast while I was still half-tangled in the hammock. Two more men came out of the darkness—I should have known; he was never alone, never—and even though one of them took hold of my legs and the other bound my arms in his strong grip and they lifted me bodily off the floor and moved me toward the mouth of the cave, even as they manhandled and bruised me, I was grateful for their presence. I knew now what I feared John would do if we were alone, what I'd always feared. I knew at last why I'd left him, and what the shape of my nightmares had been.

I only wished to the Lady and Lord that I didn't.

I struggled against John's thugs, but they didn't even seem to notice. They carried me as lightly as if the blankets that bound me were empty.

Outside I met a new horror: a blaze of red and yellow, of gold stained through with blood. So bright I thought for a moment it was dawn, but morning under the canopy was never so bright.

The tree houses. The trees. The whole forest.

All of it was on fire.

The smell that had made me choke . . . as soon as they carried me out, I knew it and wondered how I hadn't recognized it before, even in dream: it was smoke, black smoke that bled the air thin and made me struggle to breathe. The smoke caught the brightness of the fires and glowed red and gold, too, so that the unnatural light grew even brighter. I wanted to scream for Little Jane, Bird, the Mae, Stutely, and all the rest, just to hear their voices, just to know they still — But I wouldn't say their names, not within John's hearing, or his men's. I wouldn't risk telling him anything he didn't know.

One of the thugs heaved me over his back like a sack of grain. My head finally began to clear, and I was able to look around. I'd still been half in nightmare for those crucial minutes in the cave, and I cursed myself for my sluggishness, my fear. Could I have overcome him, if I'd only been more alert those few moments?

With my senses waking up at last, I realized something perhaps most horrible of all. I heard the harsh crackle of the fires, the crash as burned ruins of tree houses and platforms fell to the earth.

But I heard no screaming. No voices at all. Not one sound from the dozens of people who lived here with me, whom I had worked so hard to help and to protect.

Their silence made me find my own voice at last — and with my voice came my strength. "Let me go!" I yelled as loudly as I could. I heaved my bound legs and arched my back, throwing my weight so that the thug who held me stumbled. His hold loosened for just a moment, and that was long enough for me to force my knee up toward my hand inside the blanket and grab my knife. He gained hold of me again almost instantly, and I hadn't had time to pull my hand out of the blanket, but I was ready. He would put me down eventually.

"Calm yourself, Silvie, or I'll have them bind you truly," came John's deep voice from behind me. "And I can't promise they won't enjoy it."

My fingers tightened around the dagger. I felt it make a slit through the blanket, and an idea began to form in my mind.

I went limp, and the thug chuckled. I felt someone gently stroking my hair, although the man who held me kept both hands firmly on my legs and my hip.

The touch on my head was smooth, smooth as a snake. "Good girl," murmured John, low and close to my ear, so close I could feel the warmth of his breath even in the unnatural heat from the fires.

My hand on the knife tightened. "Please, John," I said. "You've found me again, as you said. Take me home, do with me whatever you like. Just don't—just don't hurt anyone else."

He laughed. "A little late for that, Silvie. Tom, set her down."

I saw my opportunity, and I made sure to keep myself

carefully limp as the stocky man dropped me roughly to the forest floor. I let my dagger slide through the blanket as I fell, and then I leapt free of it at once. I brandished my knife, ready for a fight.

I noticed something, someone, in the light of the fires overhead. A burning scrap of timber fell down and knocked Kent Mason's shoulder where he sat slumped against the trunk of a tree. But he didn't move, even when the flame from the wood began to lick up his sleeve. He didn't blink. He just kept staring ahead. A dark wetness bloomed on his chest where an arrow had pierced him.

That moment of shock, of immobility, cost me dear. The knife trembled in my hand, my secret exposed, and I couldn't move quickly enough to act on it.

It was bright enough from the forest fire that I could see men all around us, uniformed soldiers to one side, the silver stars on their black crests gleaming in the firelight, their eyes hard beneath metal helmets. So many of them, and Kent dead, and who knew how many others, and the houses, all the tree houses, all the forest burning. I could see a new, harsh light coming from the cave, too, brighter than Bird's fire had ever been.

Bird. Thank the Lady and Lord he had left—

But even as I had the thought, I saw him, too, bound to a tree not far away.

"Bird!" I cried, my voice a smoke-strangled rasp. He

moved, thank the Lady and Lord: he jerked against his bonds and looked up at me.

"Lord, John, she's hardly going to come quiet no matter what you think," I vaguely heard one of his men saying. "Don't you think we should—"

"Fine." Footsteps approached me from behind, but I couldn't bother to think of them, to think of anything but Kent, and to wonder how many others . . .

John's thug hit me, and I felt myself falling.

# ~EIGHTEEN~

## *Oubliette*

I wasn't bound.

That was the first thing I knew as I came back to consciousness, wincing at the headache the blow had given me. I thought I might have awakened before and been struck again, even several times, but it was hard, so hard, to tell nightmare from waking . . .

No. The pain I felt all over my body was specific and sharp and throbbing and very real. I was awake now. I could be sure of at least that much.

But I couldn't tell where I was. My eyes were open, but the place where I found myself was so dark that it made little difference. I was leaning against a hard, curved, slimy surface, so cold it stole the heat from my body. Stone: a wall of stone blocks.

I tried to push myself up to sitting; my limbs were oddly arranged, my left arm and leg twisted underneath me. Both were numb, and as the blood rushed back into them with my movements they flooded with pain.

The smell in this place was far worse than anything at Woodshire's jail. The scent of death packed the dark air, heavy as dirt.

Something crunched underneath me as I moved; while the walls were clearly stone, parts of the floor felt soft, almost malleable. My fingers dragged through something yielding and spongy.

My eyes were adjusting: I could see the faint, still outlines of several people around me. There seemed to be one faint source of light far above us, filtering weakly into the darkness.

"Silvie," came a quiet voice nearby.

One of the figures moved. I flinched, but with the first touch of his hand I knew it was Bird.

"Silvie," he said again. "I'm here. I'm with you. Try not to be afraid."

But I could see better through the gloom with every passing moment, and I could not contain my fear.

There was no one else in this small dark, dank space with Bird and me. No one else living. The other figures were corpses.

Some were barely more than skeletons, the spongy resistance I'd felt the last remnants of flesh hanging off their bones. Some were almost human-looking still, their bodies nearly in one piece but emaciated, starved, their faces slick and leathery and rotting. All dead. All dead.

I began to scream.

I went on screaming screaming screaming, because at least that took up part of the space in my mind, space that was filling with the understanding, as certain and irreversible as rising floodwater, of what had happened to the bodies around me, of what was going to happen to Bird and me, of where we were.

This was John's oubliette: the bottle-shaped dungeon he'd vowed to reopen when he became sheriff.

No one ever left an oubliette. It was in the name: you were put there to be forgotten.

My screams started to die away, and I listened to them as if from outside my body, as if the ragged sounds came from someone else.

"Silvie." Bird kept saying that name, quietly, calmly, the way he would speak to a spooked animal, keeping his hand on the screaming girl's arm. "Silvie, Silvie."

I did not want to come back to myself. To this place.

And yet, in this stone hole gouged into the earth, I needed to feel the touch of someone I loved.

Slowly, I let myself feel his hand on me, even though it meant that I also had to feel the panicked juddering of my rib cage, the shaking that rattled me to the ends of my limbs and hair and teeth. Worst of all, I had to feel the give and crunch of the floor beneath me, and know that it was made of the remains of yet more, older corpses, and of whatever slime and moss and fungus could grow on such sustenance in the darkness.

Everyone who had been tossed like refuse into this hole in the earth had died of starvation, if they had not first dashed their heads on stone walls or bone, if they were not poisoned by eating the gray mushrooms I could see growing out of the corpses' flesh, or, out of madness or desperation, by eating the flesh itself . . .

In which of those ways would I die? And Bird?

"Silvie, Silvie." My name was losing its meaning with each of Bird's repetitions, but it was, if not a comfort, the closest thing there was to comfort in this place.

"Bird." Giving his name back to him somehow made mine have meaning again. I was still myself, still someone I knew, and someone Bird knew, too. We did not share the fate of the others in this death-steeped place, not yet. Not yet.

I gripped his arm with both hands, and I managed to slow my breathing until it matched his, until we could breathe as one body in the darkness, our heads bent close together so that beyond or above the stench of death, we could take in, at least a little, the scent of the other person, still whole. Still living.

I drank in his—fresh wood and lanolin—as if it could keep me alive. Bird had always smelled good to me.

"They tell me you've woken," came a voice from above us.

I looked up at our one source of dim light: the narrow opening perhaps twenty feet above us, at the top of this bottle-shaped dungeon. The light that filtered down was flickering, surely from torches. John's face appeared as he leaned over to look at us.

"I've always been gentle with you, Silvie, always been kind. I know that you know I haven't been that way with everyone." His voice was quiet, reflective; I believed he really thought it was gentle. "I would always have been gentle with you."

I felt sick. Every cell in my body recoiled from him, even when recoiling meant pushing myself farther back into the dungeon.

"How many times did you come into my room at night, John? How many nights did you watch me sleep?"

John's mouth tightened. "I never touched you, Silvie."

I met his eyes. I knew he was telling the truth, and I could see the honesty and the lie at once, the threat that he'd never let himself carry out.

"But it was always there, wasn't it?" I already knew the answer.

"What, Silvie? That I love you? Yes, that's always, always been there."

I was starting to lose my breath again.

"You don't love her." Bird's voice was loud and harsh and steady. "Silvie, he never, never loved you. Only thought he owned you. Silvie."

My head was buzzing. John owned me now, would own me forever, would keep me here, where no one but he could find me, until I starved and died and dissolved into mold and dust . . .

I could feel nightmares closing in again, and I felt myself begin to shake . . . Who stood over me in the darkness? Who was dead in the ground, and who was living?

Someone kicked me, hard, in the leg.

Not John. He was right: he was always gentle.

It was Bird. I forced myself to be fully awake, to see him. He was glaring at me with his fiercest and angriest look, the one most like his falcon's.

I swallowed. My world came into focus again.

Meanwhile, John was going on as if Bird hadn't spoken at all. "I have done nothing to you, ever, Silvie, that you didn't want done," he said. His voice echoed strangely through the oubliette's narrow neck. "I never wanted to take from you anything you didn't want to give. I just hoped that maybe, if I waited . . . There is no sin in wanting, Silvie. But you, you wanted . . . squalor. Wilderness. Chaos. *Him.*"

I was looking at Bird, because otherwise I would have

to look at something dead, or at John. I was looking at only my Bird: my friend since childhood, my companion, my salvation.

John was right. I had always wanted Bird.

"There's no sin in wanting," John repeated. "But what you've done, Silvie—not just wanted, but done—that's sin indeed. Putting you down there was the only way to save you from it."

"Let Bird go, John." There was no way out for me, not any longer. I had only one weapon left, and John, whether he knew it or not, had provided it. "Let him go, and I'll— I'll come home. I'll stay with you, be with you." Loughsley Abbey, walled gardens, dark libraries, the prison I'd spent my whole childhood loving, not knowing the ghosts that we fed on . . . and John, John in every corner, watching, waiting, wanting, every day, and every night . . .

"Let him go, John, and I'll come home with you, and we'll be together."

"Stop, Silvie, stop—" Bird's voice was losing its steadiness, but John cut him off before he could go on.

"It's too late for that, Silvie. I told you, I know. I know why you left with him." I could hear the vicious assurance in his voice. "You were always the weaker of us, Silvie. I've spent my life resisting your temptations, and you—you run off to rut with serfs in the forest at the first opportunity."

I had to stare up at him then. He was watching me, his face calm at first glance but violent in its depths, the face he had always had. "You're offering me spoiled goods, Silvie. The only thing you've given to the poor is your virtue, and you've gotten nothing back."

"I was happy, John, in the forest. I belonged to myself, and to people I love. I only wanted to help them belong to themselves, too."

He scoffed. "Belong to themselves? Everyone who joined you in the forest is dead, Silvie. Every one of them but you. It was you who killed them, really, by letting them think they could escape the king. You lied to them all. This trick you pulled with the palace stores—no one will even know it was you. The king and I have forbidden anyone to speak your name, to mention the Forest Queen. You won't even be a story. *Oubliette* means 'forgotten,' did you know that? I have you somewhere now that only I know about, and only I will remember you." My brother stood up, and his face vanished from the small circle of the dungeon's opening. "He may have claimed your body, but I have both your souls."

I heard his steps grow fainter, until Bird and I were utterly alone.

My eyes were stinging; my mouth was dry.

"They're all dead."

Bird and the corpses watched me.

"It was cruel of me to say I could help them," I said. "I didn't help. I turned them into revolutionaries, just like Ghazia said. I turned them into people their kingdom thought they could kill." I raised my hands to wipe my tears, but remembered the slime and rot they'd just trailed through and recoiled from myself.

"Silvie, you freed them. Everyone who came to live with us. The men in Woodshire Jail. Mae Tuck. Little Jane."

"Don't say their names." I saw Little Jane burning in my mind. John had taken everything from her after all; neither of us had gotten free of him, and she had died in pain, burning, burning. And Anna Robin—

I couldn't. I couldn't think of it.

"Bird, they're all dead. I never helped them. I only brought them to ruin. My life, my . . . death—it doesn't matter. All of their lives, all of their hopes, the hopes I sold them—they burned away. That matters."

"Right." Bird stood, yanking me up with him. Our feet sank into the murky filth, crunched on decaying bones. "Right. Silvie, by the Lady and Lord, you won't die believing you failed." He glared at me, fixed and determined. "You—you and I and Little Jane, and all of our band together—we proved that there's a different way to live, and we taught everyone how to live it. Not just the family we made in the forest, but . . . Do you think anyone will stop telling their story, our story, because of John's threats? The whole country knows now, Silvie, that there are other choices than the life the nobles hand to you. Knows that it's possible to help ourselves and help each other. John has made us martyrs now, every one of us. Everyone who died in the forest." Bird was faltering, his eyes glancing around at the inevitable death that surrounded us, but I watched as he steeled himself again, looking into my eyes. "He's lost his own war, and it's his hand that did it. Silvie, they'll never stop telling your story."

It was clear he believed what he said. Here in the darkness, he had found some light to reflect back to me, however faint. He was giving me a gift.

What else could I do, at the end of my life, but make the choice to take it?

I closed my eyes, nodding. I wanted to believe, I chose to believe, that he was right.

"Why did you leave, Bird?" I whispered. "After the May dance, where did you go?"

He shook his head, his forehead resting against mine. "I'm so sorry, Silvie. I wish I'd never gone."

"It doesn't matter now, I know. Not here. But . . ."

"I was angry. I saw you pulling away, saw that *never* look

in your eyes while we were dancing, and it was one time too many. I didn't think I could stay without . . . asking more of you than you wanted to give." He sighed. "I didn't want to bind you, when you'd done so much to gain freedom. I was selfish, Silvie. I was weak. I see that now. I saw it almost right away—that's why I came back."

"You came back? I couldn't find you . . ."

He shook his head. "I couldn't face you yet. I thought I'd have time, that we'd have so much time to talk these things through. But John found us, of course. Found all of us. I saw him and his men enter the clearing, with Nell and Nellie Mason held at knifepoint."

I flinched. "I thought you'd left with Nellie."

"Nellie? Oh, Silvie. I've only ever—" he stopped himself. "I know it's not what you wanted, but I only ever wanted you."

I opened my eyes again.

He had given me a gift, but there was another that I wanted to take, or to give.

We'd had so much time, Bird and I. Almost all of our lives. I had spent that time refusing the part of him I wanted most, holding back the part of myself I most wanted to share.

I had gone with him to the forest, but I had not reached out for the life we might have had together. I had been afraid that I would lose it. Lose him.

Now we had no forest to roam, no secret chair at the garden's edge, no firelit cave, no life to look forward to at all, together or apart. We had nothing before us but death.

I couldn't kiss him passionately. Not here, not in this place.

But I could put my arms around him, put my lips to his forehead, his cheeks, his lips, and give all of myself to that touch.

I felt the weight and warmth of all our shared years in his body and mine as we broke our old promise. He kissed me back, and I knew he felt it, too.

A fire that never went out. An unbridled, unending love.

Here, at the end of our lives, we gave, and took, the only thing we had left.

❦ ❦

After our one, quiet kiss, as we huddled together in the dark, I do not know how much time passed. I kept remembering Anna Robin's birth, that timeless space where we waited for new life to come, a bright inverse of this dark place where we waited for death. Time had seemed to stop then, too.

As much as I tried to push Little Jane and Anna Robin from my mind, they haunted me. The first two lives I had tried, and failed, to save.

We didn't speak of them anymore—we couldn't—but

I knew they haunted Bird, too, their ghosts as present in the oubliette as the flesh and bone around us.

We clung to each other every minute, every second, of that endless time. Bird wanted to believe that we could find a way out, an escape, if we tried hard enough: and so we paced our cell, stepping over bodies where we could avoid them, running our hands over the smooth, cold, terrible slime of the concave stone walls, looking for a foothold, a fissure, anything.

There was nothing.

"Of course there isn't!" I cried, at the end of an hour or a night or a week of desperate, repetitive searching and trying and working to find a way to survive. We had tied our clothes together to form a rope, but there was nothing to attach it to. We had tried, the Lady and Lord forgive us, to build a ladder of bones. They cracked and crumbled in our hands.

"If there were any way out, Bird, one of these people would have found it. We had to try, I know. Just to keep from going mad. But there's nothing. Nothing."

Bird didn't speak. He stared up at the faint circle of light above us, his face already thinner than it had been when I had woken to find us here, his skin sallow and tight, and slick with the stale moisture of the air.

He sank down, his back sliding against the wall. We still held each other's hands—aside from when we were knotting or building, we'd hardly let go of each other for a moment since I'd kissed him, even in sleep—but there was no strength at all left in his grip, and barely any warmth. He looked at the light above us with a blank despair, like a wild creature that finally understands it has been caged.

I sat down next to him, moved my hand up his arm to his neck, and gently moved his head to rest it on my shoulder.

He shivered weakly, but he took the support I offered.

"Try to sleep, Bird," I said. "At least we can escape that way."

I knew that madness was coming for us; that, presented with the choice between insanity and watching Bird and myself slowly starve in the dark, my mind would choose the former. I was nearly looking forward to that escape.

So I felt no surprise when an angel appeared above me.

I thought it was my first vision. It glowed the way an angel is supposed to glow, and it was beautiful and strange, the way angels are said to be. It even had feathered wings.

If this was a vision, a hallucination, I welcomed it with gratitude.

The angel's wings sparked in the dim light as it descended from heaven into our pit, and its feathers, or its eyes, seemed to glow with a yellow light of their own.

The angel landed on my knee. Its talons scratched me.

"Hello," I said to the angel. "Mae Tuck must have had the Lady send you."

Its face, round and snowy white, was lovely.

It leaned forward and pecked my cheek.

"Ow!" I slapped it away.

The angel glared at me with its yellow eyes. It squawked. It hooted.

My thin, starved blood began to rush fast through my veins, my weakened heart to pump quickly with joy.

This was no angel, no vision, no madness.

It was my owl.

I scrabbled up to standing. "Bird!"

He'd obeyed my instructions to sleep, and he rose sluggishly, but when he saw Scarlet, he gasped and stared.

"Tie something to her leg," he said at once. "A piece of clothing, a—"

I took a lock of my long hair in my mouth and bit it off. I fixed it around Scarlet's leg with shaking hands.

John had said he'd killed them all, every one, in the forest. But how could he know for sure? How could we know?

And what could we do but seize the one strange, small hope presented to us?

Scarlet didn't want to leave us. I had to practically toss her upward to get her to fly away.

Maybe she wouldn't go back to the forest, now that it

was burned. Maybe there would be no one there to find her, no one for her to find.

But there might be.

We waited.

And then . . . an hour, a night, or a week later . . .

Scarlet came back. In place of the lock of hair I'd tied to her, there was a small and tightly rolled scroll of paper.

There was only one line, hard to make out in the gloom despite the clear handwriting. I knew that handwriting, I thought . . .

"Mae Tuck," Bird whispered, reaching out to touch the paper delicately, as if he thought it might melt in his hand. I remembered her neatly labeled vials of medicine, and I began to weep with gratitude, with the lifted weight of grief taken away.

Mae Tuck lived.

John had lied.

And surely others had survived, too. For the paper read: *We are coming. Take heart.*

# ~NINETEEN~
## The Forest Queen

The following days were closer to nightmare than any others we'd spent in the ground. When you think death is inevitable, part of you, some bone-deep animal part, wants to lie down and accept it.

When you have hope, even a tiny and absurd hope, the human part of you will scrabble after it until your last breath.

We had no respite, not even a moment of the escape of sleep, for the rest of our time in that place.

I could count the days that passed, because Scarlet came back to us regularly, at the beginning of what I soon realized was each morning, and she stayed, sleeping in the prison with us, until what must have been nightfall.

The second time she came, Seraph followed. She cooed and rubbed her head against Bird's cheek, sweet as a dove. Bird roused himself enough to pet her, his hand trembling, but when she flew away his expression was more despairing than ever.

On the third day, Much was with them, bearing a trout the length of my hand clutched in his beak, its red gills still fluttering. Bird and I ate it raw.

I tried not to cling to any hope that Much's survival meant that Little Jane had lived, too. Owls could fly above a fire.

I tried not to fix myself with too much certainty to the hope that Mae Tuck and whoever else was left, the "we" she wrote of, would truly be able to find us. I had no idea where we were in the vast prison grounds that John had reopened. I had no idea how many guards were posted around us; certainly no one had responded, or made any noise at all, when Bird and I had tried to shout for help.

The fourth day, Scarlet brought a rope.

She dove into the cave with its end clasped in her beak and dropped it, flying out to freedom again at once.

I stared at it. Grasped it. The slender length of hemp felt rough and light in my hands. My eyes followed it up, up, and out of the oubliette.

Bird was staring, grasping, too. Together we pulled on the rope, and we brought in maybe ten feet of slack before it pulled taut.

There was no discussion, no question of trust for the rope or whoever had sent it, no wondering about tricks. Whatever waited at the other end of that line was better than the oubliette.

We only nodded to each other, and I began to climb. When I let go of Bird to grasp the rope with both hands, it was the first time we'd stopped touching in days. Losing that connection was more than startling, more than frightening. I never wanted to lose it again.

The oubliette tapered until its walls brushed my shoulders as I climbed. Strange furry mosses, condensation, more pale little fungi brushed against and seeped into my damp clothes. The air got colder as I moved farther upward, away from the heat of decomposition we'd lived in for days or weeks. My clothes grew colder, too, clammy with slime and dew, and they stuck to my skin. I felt my hair pasted to my cheeks and neck and shoulders as if I'd been swimming.

When I finally pulled myself out, it was like swimming, too, like coming up for breath after too long underwater. The absence of the terrible smell was a miracle. I gasped and fell forward, digging my fingers into the dirt.

I turned around and offered my hand to Bird. The narrow opening was an even tighter fit for him, and I grasped his arm and helped him pull himself out, first one shoulder, then the other.

Kneeling at the edge of the oubliette, taking desperate, gulping breaths, he looked like someone brought back from the dead. I knew I must look the same.

I wanted to embrace him, but we could not waste this

chance we had been given. We shouldn't have even taken the moments we had.

I stood and looked around, ready to see a guard or a battalion of soldiers or even John himself emerge from the dark expanse around us, the barred cells that I could just barely make out forming a rough square around our prison, around at least ten identical holes in the ground. I reeled, thinking of all the bodies inside them, all the miserable, drawn-out deaths over the centuries. A horrible secret that our kingdom had all but forgotten, until my brother brought it back.

A voice in the shadows: "Forest Queen!"

I startled and turned toward the sound. One fluid shadow moved slightly, a silent black-robed form.

Ghazia. The Su princess had an unconscious guard under each foot.

"Are you well enough to walk on your own?" she asked. "I thought I might have to go down there to get you. I had to convince them not to come barging in after you, once your owls led us here. They are so desperate to see you safe. Here, come out of the light."

The light Ghazia spoke of was just a few torches, but we obeyed her quickly.

"Who?" I whispered. I was glad, grateful beyond reckoning, to see Ghazia and to have her help, but . . . I had not known her long. Hers was not one of the faces of our forest family that I longed so badly to see, that I had felt so certain I would never see again.

One of the guards under Ghazia's feet began to stir. She knocked him out again with a swift and precise jab of her heel, but she shook her head at me and her meaning was clear: *Not now.* First we had to get out.

We slipped after her through one room, then another, following the rope the whole time. We moved as quickly as our weakened states would let us. I wanted Bird to go in front of me, to take the protected center position in our trio, but as pale and trembling as he was, he used whatever stubbornness he had left to absolutely refuse. So I looked back at him as often as I could let myself as we made our way out, and out, and out. Often I thought I saw shapes moving in the shadows, perhaps even recognized the form of someone I might know, one of the rogues, maybe—even, once, I was almost sure, Nellie Mason.

But I thought I saw movement dozens of times, a hundred times, more. Our group had never been so numerous, even before John's massacre.

I knew I was only seeing ghosts.

We breached three sets of walls before we were outside the prison doors themselves. So much of my strength had drained away in our endless time in the oubliette that every one of them felt like climbing a mountain.

The prison sat outside Esting City proper, which meant

that—just like every other bit of civilization our country had eked out—it was on the edge of the forest. Shrubs and brambles crowded in on the old stone walls, and tall pine and oak and beech trees began to rise just a few steps ahead of us.

And there, under the branches of an oak tree, was a figure I would always recognize, that I could never mistake for anyone else. Little Jane stood tall and watchful, holding a solid, long staff, Anna Robin sleeping on her chest. Beside her stood Mae Tuck.

Not ghosts. Not shadows. Nothing but themselves, three people, living and breathing.

I tried to embrace them all at once. I was shaking, laughing. Relieved beyond the power of word or gesture to express.

"You're alive," I rasped into Little Jane's shoulder. "You're still alive."

I looked at the sleeping baby, her pudgy mouth relaxed into almost perfect roundness, impossibly long eyelashes casting their own faint shadows on her full cheeks. Her perfect, smooth, unburned skin. The miraculous tiny in-and-out sweep of her breaths.

"How did you survive the fire, the ambush? How many lived?" I asked, stepping back. I turned my gaze to Mae Tuck. "John said you all died. He said he and his men killed you all."

The Mae, somber, shook her head. "Kent Mason. Simon Warden. Arthur Tailor. Susan and Eric Caprin, the sweet boy, and his goats."

"Silvie . . ." Bird said behind me, his hand still touching my back.

"I need to know." But Mae Tuck had said something that didn't make sense. "I saw Kent, when John took me. I saw him with an arrow through his chest. How could he have lived?"

The Mae looked at me searchingly. "He didn't, child. These are the names of the dead." She made the Lady's sign on her chest.

I stared. "So few?"

"You underestimate your people, Forest Queen." Ghazia's voice was low and steady. I turned to look at her, and I was more shocked than I'd yet been that night.

A horde stood behind her.

"We had to breach the prison in layers, and every single person we freed remained with us to join our numbers, to overpower the guards. By the time we got to you in the oubliette, we had an army."

Some clearly had been prisoners of the jail we'd just left, wearing ragged clothes and haggard expressions, their bodies thin and malnourished. Dozens more were members of our forest family: rogues, refugees, women and men, and even some of the older youths. Will Stutely stood among them, that smile flashing through his thick beard. He walked up to Bird and they clasped hands, sharing a look of intense relief.

There were even nobles among the crowd: several more Su dignitaries, who must have followed Ghazia. Clara was there, with three of the ladies I'd seen wearing almond blossoms at the May Festival.

And hundreds, hundreds, of commoners stood with them. Villagers, farmers, merchants, palace servants still in uniform. Half the population of Esting, I thought, must be there.

"What is this?" I whispered. Then, louder: "What are they all doing here? They're all in danger now! What if John comes?"

"In danger?" Alana Dale stepped out of the crowd, carrying her lute. "There are more of us here than there are soldiers in the palace, not that my lady Ghazia could not dispatch them single-handed." She gave a little bow to the princess, who raised her hand to her veil as if to hide a blush.

"And John," Little Jane said grimly, "is here."

I started in fright, but Little Jane laid a hand on my shoulder and pointed to a tree a small distance away from us, where several rogues stood at guard, brandishing knives or staffs. When they parted, I could see my brother, tied to the tree, his face tight with pain or rage.

"They wanted to kill him," Little Jane said. "I wanted to kill him myself, or at least, part of me did." She touched the sleeping Anna's head. "But he's your kin, Silvie. I thought . . . you should decide."

I walked up to John, the lord of Loughsley, the sheriff. The bully, the rapist, the murderer, who managed to think himself virtuous because there was one sin he'd never let himself commit. I remembered all the nights at Loughsley that he stood by my bed, radiating his longing to touch me, and how that longing had poisoned my dreams. I remembered his voice, its sinuous calmness, above us in the oubliette. I remembered how he left us there to die.

He had raped Little Jane. He had stolen her family from her, her place in the village. He had made her want to die, had taken a part of her soul that it took months in the forest, months of work and rest and hunting and building and freedom, and the birth of Anna Robin, for her to begin to restore in herself. I remembered every day, every bit of suffering, that went into the redemption my friend had found.

For some reason I remembered the hart on the day of the Hunt Ball, how he had let it suffer to ingratiate himself with our prince. I remembered how he had hit us, the day I met Bird. I remembered my brother at eight years old, crushing blackbird chicks under his boots.

I faced each of those memories. When the face of my brother before me made me wish to show him mercy, I kept facing each memory of his cruelty, his violence, and I did not let myself forget.

"The oubliette," I said. "You said you wanted to keep me there so that the world would forget me. So that only you would remember."

His face grew pale.

"No one deserves to die in such a way, in such a place," I said. "Almost no one."

The blackbird chicks. The wounded stag. The legions of people John had taxed past bearing, had bullied, had tortured. Little Jane hanging from the Wedding-Ring Bridge.

The crowd stood around us, waiting, watching.

*We should put him down there,* I thought, *and forget him.*

"Little Jane," I said.

She was before me in a moment, her head high, her glare as fierce as Bird's. There wasn't a trace of fear in her eyes as she looked at John.

"I told him I wanted to kill him," I said, "and I do. But I don't think I can want it as much as you do."

I took one step back from my brother and gestured for my friend to take my place.

"Her, Silvie?" he hissed, low words just meant for my ears. "Silvie, she doesn't matter . . ."

I tightened my grip. "She matters."

Little Jane moved toward him, her own garter-knife raised in her hand. "Don't I, just," she said. She was looking at John, but for a moment our eyes met over his shoulder, and I remembered our meeting at the bridge, our first night in the forest, every night since. The night of Anna Robin's birth.

"We all of us matter," Little Jane said. "Even you." She put the knife to his throat, but didn't press; she dragged it down, slowly, to his panting belly. "I've a baby from you, you know. A daughter."

"I have a baby?"

"You don't," I said. "Little Jane does. You've no right even to know about her baby, unless she says so. You've no right even to know her name."

"Don't be absurd, Silvie, a nameless bastard—" His words cut off in a ragged cry.

Little Jane lowered her knife.

"I don't want him to die," she said in response to my questioning look. "I just want him to know. And I want him to live to remember it, the way I have. The way you have."

We did. We neither of us feared him anymore, but I knew we would always remember.

"We'll put it to a vote," I said. "It's the only just thing."

I knew I was right even before I saw the sudden rising fear in John's eyes; but I admit I savored seeing it nonetheless.

At the front of the circle of torches, I saw Bird nod.

In the end, we put it to a vote, and the people chose to

put John in the old Woodshire Jail. He wouldn't be alone there, either; for the one or two prisoners whom Simon and Stutely had believed really were too cruel to mix among free society were still there. They'd be apt company for John, at least, I thought.

Several of the rogues bore John away. I think he was screaming, beneath his gag, but the sound was too muffled to know for sure.

❧ ❧

"Why did they come, all those people?" I asked as we walked back through the forest. The endless time in the oubliette had left me weak, and I leaned on Little Jane for support. Bird limped along on her other side, and she helped him walk, too. Looking at us, anyone would think she had always been the rescuer; and at that moment, I felt that she had.

A wet smell of old smoke tamped down by rain hung in the air. We had crossed the edge of the fire's destruction, and burned trees creaked around us. Damp ashes stuck to the soles of our shoes, kicked up around the hems of our cloaks.

"They love you, Silvie," Little Jane said. "The money and supplies you set loose on the river that night fed the whole kingdom. John said you died, and that made you a martyr. I never believed it, though, Silvie. Never. When

Scarlet brought back your hair . . ." She shivered. "I feel my life tied to yours now, ever since you saved me, and more since Anna Robin was born. You saved the people, too, and so their lives are tied to yours. John and the king's taxes had them on the edge of oblivion, and you saved them all. Just like you saved me."

I shook my head. We'd pulled Little Jane off the bridge and brought her to the forest, but she had made the choice to live, to go on, every day after that. "We only gave them back what should never have been taken away. And how did they know, anyway, that I had anything to do with it?"

"You'd be surprised how quickly a ballad can spread through a city, a forest, a country, if its story is good enough," said Alana Dale. She winked at me. "And if it's well sung."

She hummed a few bars, and began to sing. Little Jane, to my surprise, sang with her; just ahead of us, so did Mae Tuck.

> *Come listen to me, you who wish to be free,*
> *If you love a good tale to hear,*
> *And I will tell you of the Forest Queen*
> *Who lives in wild Woodshire . . .*

The words were Alana's, of course, but it was an old tune, used in innumerable ballads.

Bird began to hum along. Mae Tuck's strong alto voice, and Jane's softer one, rose with Alana's and echoed through the trees around us.

The song grew louder, much louder than three or four voices . . .

All around us, the people of Esting were singing, too. I couldn't see them through the burned yet still-standing trees. But I could hear them, their rushing, rising harmony, singing the words of Alana's ballad as if they'd known them all their lives.

"I told you they'd always tell your story," Bird whispered in my ear.

I shook my head, unutterably humbled, and grateful, and proud.

And the song went on.

Summer

# Epilogue

A burned forest is reborn in flowers.

Where once the leaves and needles of ancient oaks and pine trees shadowed the ground, suddenly sunlight has room to stream down, to stroke its gold fingers across the scorched earth. Ashes melt into and feed the soil. Underground, seeds uncurl, life in the wake of death. Shoots push fragile into the air, aiming for sky. Some will blossom and fade by the summer's end; some will become trees, great elder rulers of the forest, and in two hundred years they will still offer shade and shelter.

The day I married Bird, flowers covered the world.

It was Midsummer Day. Three-year-old Anna Robin embodied her role as flower girl absolutely: a frothy circle of meadowsweet crowned her hair, cornflowers and asters were pinned to her white linen dress, and she carried a wicker basket of wild rose petals that was half as tall as she was. Showing signs of her mother's strength already, she wielded the huge basket with determination and threw petals in the face of anyone who crossed her path, shrieking with glee.

Little Jane watched her with gentle amusement from her place by my side on the Wedding-Ring Bridge. With a bouquet of dahlias and a crown to match her daughter's in her hair, she made a beautiful maid of honor. Even Scarlet and Much were in attendance: the owls often roosted in the covered bridge during summer. Today Alana's music, and everyone's merry laughter, had shaken them out of their daytime sleep, and they glared at us from the shadows of the rafters. Seraph had found her perch with Bird's mother. She sat erect on the huntmistress's shoulder, and both of them watched us with a fierce, sharp, and undeniable pride.

Mae Tuck held a bouquet of her own instead of a prayer book as she presided over the ceremony — although she had to hold it in one arm when Anna Robin tugged at her skirt, asking to be held. The toddler beamed at us as the Mae spoke of holy days, of turning points in the wheel of the year.

"Today marks the beginning of a new season," she said, "for the earth, and for you. The warmth of summer, the harvest in autumn, the restful stillness of winter, and the resurrection of spring bring blessings for the earth and all who walk upon it. So may you bring blessings to each other, through all the seasons of your lives."

Bird clasped my waist and pulled me close. I drank in his kiss like a tree drinks in sunlight.

I heard a whistle from the crowd below—Will Stutely, surely—and we parted, laughing.

I tossed my armful of lilies over the balustrade and the river caught it. The white bundle danced on the water, the flowers scattering with each ripple and wave.

My hands free, I grasped Bird on my right side and Little Jane on my left, and we ran off the bridge and into the welcoming crowd.

# Author's Note

Come listen to me, you gallants so free,
All you that love mirth for to hear,
And I will you tell of a bold outlaw,
That lived in Nottinghamshire.
— "Robin Hood and Allen a Dale"
*English and Scottish Popular Ballads,*
ed. Francis James Child, 1888

Most historians these days will tell you that Robin Hood never existed. Even when he was generally believed to have lived at one point or another, it was hard for anyone to agree on who he was, or even what century he lived in. The fact that he was a "he" was pretty much the only constant. However, just as Silvie comes to care about the liberation of her community more than her own life, knowing the ideals behind Robin Hood lore is more important than knowing whether such a person really walked through Sherwood Forest. The radical rejection of an unjust system, stealing from the rich to give to the poor, is an inspiring notion regardless of historical veracity.

Alana Dale is the only character in this book who is based on a real person: Julie d'Aubigny, "La Maupin." La Maupin was an opera star and swordswoman in seventeenth-century France, as famous for her many duels and her love affairs with both men and women as for her beautiful voice. She really did join a nunnery under false pretenses, to free her imprisoned lover—an adventure that involved bodysnatching, arson, and a sentence to death by fire. Alana's songs, "The Maid Freed from the Gallows" in Chapter 15 and a slightly altered "Robin Hood and Allen a Dale" at the book's end, are real folk ballads.

Loughsley Abbey is real, too, or at least, it's based on Kylemore Abbey in Connemara, Ireland. The lordly "big house" set between a rockface and a river, complete with a sophisticated-for-its-time running-water system and beautiful walled gardens, is one of Ireland's most famous buildings for good reason (although its real-life owners seem to have been at least a little kinder to the people around them than the Loughsleys were).

Since there are female versions of Allen a Dale (Alana), the Saracen (Ghazia), Friar Tuck (Mae Tuck), and Little John (Little Jane), as well as Robin, in this book, it might seem strange that there's no male Maid Marian here. In my research, I was surprised to learn that Maid Marian is absent from the earliest known recordings of the Robin Hood ballads. When she does first appear, it's as a personification of the Virgin Mary, or of pagan May Day festivities; she did not become Robin's love interest until Victorian times. In some early stories, Robin Hood was himself a "Marian," a follower of Mary. I wanted to bring back that veneration of the divine feminine in my own retelling.

I had my first baby while writing *The Forest Queen,* and I received wise and compassionate care from the midwives in Ireland's public health-care system, as well as from COPE Galway's Waterside House. Mae Tuck is all the women who guided me so kindly and expertly through the earthshaking transition to motherhood. I am so grateful to them, and also to two old friends who work in the field: Emma Dorsey, who helped me find information on midwifery, birth control, and abortion in medieval and Renaissance Europe, and Katherin Hudkins, a postpartum doula who crossed an ocean to bring her support to my family. The word *Mae* is applied to holy women in several religious traditions, including the Mae chee in Thai Buddhism and the Mãe-de-santo in Umbanda, and I borrow it here with heartfelt respect.

*The Forest Queen* is dedicated to my baby. I love you beyond the measure of any words.